T0144325

The Dorrington Deed-Box

The Dorrington Deed-Box

Arthur Morrison

MINT EDITIONS

The Dorrington Deed-Box was first published in 1897.

This edition published by Mint Editions 2021.

ISBN 9781513207421 | E-ISBN 9781513285801

Published by Mint Editions®

MINT
EDITIONS

minteditionbooks.com

Publishing Director: Jennifer Newens
Design & Production: Rachel Lopez Metzger
Project Manager: Micaela Clark
Typesetting: Westchester Publishing Services

Contents

I. The Narrative of Mr. James Rigby   7

II. The Case of Janissary   30

III. The Case of the "Mirror of Portugal"   51

IV. The Affair of the "Avalanche Bicycle
and Tyre Co., Limited"   73

V. The Case of Mr. Loftus Deacon   94

VI. Old Cater's Money   119

I

The Narrative of Mr. James Rigby

I shall here set down in language as simple and straightforward as I can command, the events which followed my recent return to England; and I shall leave it to others to judge whether or not my conduct has been characterised by foolish fear and ill-considered credulity. At the same time I have my own opinion as to what would have been the behaviour of any other man of average intelligence and courage in the same circumstances; more especially a man of my exceptional upbringing and retired habits.

I was born in Australia, and I have lived there all my life till quite recently, save for a single trip to Europe as a boy, in company with my father and mother. It was then that I lost my father. I was less than nine years old at the time, but my memory of the events of that European trip is singularly vivid.

My father had emigrated to Australia at the time of his marriage, and had become a rich man by singularly fortunate speculations in land in and about Sydney. As a family we were most uncommonly self-centred and isolated. From my parents I never heard a word as to their relatives in England; indeed to this day I do not as much as know what was the Christian name of my grandfather. I have often supposed that some serious family quarrel or great misfortune must have preceded or accompanied my father's marriage. Be that as it may, I was never able to learn anything of my relatives, either on my mother's or my father's side. Both parents, however, were educated people, and indeed I fancy that their habit of seclusion must first have arisen from this circumstance, since the colonists about them in the early days, excellent people as they were, were not as a class distinguished for extreme intellectual culture. My father had his library stocked from England, and added to by fresh arrivals from time to time; and among his books he would pass most of his days, taking, however, now and again an excursion with a gun in search of some new specimen to add to his museum of natural history, which occupied three long rooms in our house by the Lane Cove river.

I was, as I have said, eight years of age when I started with my parents on a European tour, and it was in the year 1873. We stayed but a short while in England at first arrival, intending to make a longer stay on our return from the Continent. We made our tour, taking Italy last, and it was here that my father encountered a dangerous adventure.

We were at Naples, and my father had taken an odd fancy for a picturesque-looking ruffian who had attracted his attention by a complexion unusually fair for an Italian, and in whom he professed to recognise a likeness to Tasso the poet. This man became his guide in excursions about the neighbourhood of Naples, though he was not one of the regular corps of guides, and indeed seemed to have no regular occupation of a definite sort. "Tasso," as my father always called him, seemed a civil fellow enough, and was fairly intelligent; but my mother disliked him extremely from the first, without being able to offer any very distinct reason for her aversion. In the event her instinct was proved true.

"Tasso"—his correct name, by the way, was Tommaso Marino— persuaded my father that something interesting was to be seen at the Astroni crater, four miles west of the city, or thereabout; persuaded him, moreover, to make the journey on foot; and the two accordingly set out. All went well enough till the crater was reached, and then, in a lonely and broken part of the hill, the guide suddenly turned and attacked my father with a knife, his intention, without a doubt, being murder and the acquisition of the Englishman's valuables. Fortunately my father had a hip-pocket with a revolver in it, for he had been warned of the danger a stranger might at that time run wandering in the country about Naples. He received a wound in the flesh of his left arm in an attempt to ward off a stab, and fired, at wrestling distance, with the result that his assailant fell dead on the spot. He left the place with all speed, tying up his arm as he went, sought the British consul at Naples, and informed him of the whole circumstances. From the authorities there was no great difficulty. An examination or two, a few signatures, some particular exertions on the part of the consul, and my father was free, so far as the officers of the law were concerned. But while these formalities were in progress no less than three attempts were made on his life—two by the knife and one by shooting—and in each his escape was little short of miraculous. For the dead ruffian, Marino, had been a member of the dreaded Camorra, and the Camorristi were eager to avenge his death. To anybody acquainted with the internal history of Italy—more particularly the history of the old kingdom of Naples—the name of the Camorra will be familiar enough. It was one of the worst and most powerful of the many powerful and evil secret societies of

Italy, and had none of the excuses for existence which have been from time to time put forward on behalf of the others. It was a gigantic club for the commission of crime and the extortion of money. So powerful was it that it actually imposed a regular tax on all food material entering Naples—a tax collected and paid with far more regularity than were any of the taxes due to the lawful Government of the country. The carrying of smuggled goods was a monopoly of the Camorra, a perfect organisation existing for the purpose throughout the kingdom. The whole population was terrorised by this detestable society, which had no less than twelve centres in the city of Naples alone. It contracted for the commission of crime just as systematically and calmly as a railway company contracts for the carriage of merchandise. A murder was so much, according to circumstances, with extras for disposing of the body; arson was dealt in profitably; maimings and kidnappings were carried out with promptitude and despatch; and any diabolical outrage imaginable was a mere matter of price. One of the staple vocations of the concern was of course brigandage. After the coming of Victor Emanuel and the fusion of Italy into one kingdom the Camorra lost some of its power, but for a long time gave considerable trouble. I have heard that in the year after the matters I am describing two hundred Camorristi were banished from Italy.

As soon as the legal forms were complied with, my father received the broadest possible official hint that the sooner and the more secretly he left the country the better it would be for himself and his family. The British consul, too, impressed it upon him that the law would be entirely unable to protect him against the machinations of the Camorra; and indeed it needed but little persuasion to induce us to leave, for my poor mother was in a state of constant terror lest we were murdered together in our hotel; so that we lost no time in returning to England and bringing our European trip to a close.

In London we stayed at a well-known private hotel near Bond Street. We had been but three days here when my father came in one evening with a firm conviction that he had been followed for something like two hours, and followed very skilfully too. More than once he had doubled suddenly with a view to confront the pursuers, who he felt were at his heels, but he had met nobody of a suspicious appearance. The next afternoon I heard my mother telling my governess (who was travelling with us) of an unpleasant-looking man, who had been hanging about opposite the hotel door, and who, she felt sure, had afterwards been following her and my father as they were walking. My mother grew nervous, and communicated her fears to my father. He, however, pooh-poohed the thing, and took little thought of its meaning. Nevertheless the dogging continued, and my father, who was never able to fix upon the persons who caused the annoyance—indeed he rather felt their presence by instinct, as one does in such cases, than otherwise—grew extremely angry, and had some idea of consulting the police. Then one morning my mother discovered a little paper label stuck on the outside of the door of the bedroom occupied by herself and my father. It was a small thing, circular, and about the size of a sixpenny-piece, or even smaller, but my mother was quite certain that it had not been there when she last entered the door the night before, and she was much terrified. For the label carried a tiny device, drawn awkwardly in ink—a pair of knives of curious shape, crossed: the sign of the Camorra.

Nobody knew anything of this label, or how it came where it had been found. My mother urged my father to place himself under the protection of the police at once, but he delayed. Indeed, I fancy he had a suspicion that the label might be the production of some practical joker staying at the hotel who had heard of his Neapolitan adventure (it was reported in many newspapers) and designed to give him a fright. But that very evening my poor father was found dead, stabbed in a dozen places, in a short, quiet street not forty yards from the hotel. He had merely gone out to buy a few cigars of a particular brand which he fancied, at a shop two streets away, and in less than half an hour of his departure the police were at the hotel door with the news of his death, having got his address from letters in his pockets.

It is no part of my present design to enlarge on my mother's grief, or to describe in detail the incidents that followed my father's death, for I am going back to this early period of my life merely to make more clear the bearings of what has recently happened to myself. It will be sufficient therefore to say that at the inquest the jury returned a verdict of wilful murder against some person or persons unknown; that it was several times reported that the police had obtained a most important clue, and that being so, very naturally there was never any arrest. We returned to Sydney, and there I grew up.

I should perhaps have mentioned ere this that my profession—or I should rather say my hobby—is that of an artist. Fortunately or unfortunately, as you may please to consider it, I have no need to follow any profession as a means of livelihood, but since I was sixteen years of age my whole time has been engrossed in drawing and painting. Were it not for my mother's invincible objection to parting with me, even for the shortest space of time, I should long ago have come to Europe to work and to study in the regular schools. As it was I made shift to do my best in Australia, and wandered about pretty freely, struggling with the difficulties of moulding into artistic form the curious Australian landscape. There is an odd, desolate, uncanny note in characteristic Australian scenery, which most people are apt to regard as of little value for the purposes of the landscape painter, but with which I have always been convinced that an able painter could do great things. So I did my feeble best.

Two years ago my mother died. My age was then twenty-eight, and I was left without a friend in the world, and, so far as I know, without a relative. I soon found it impossible any longer to inhabit the large house by the Lane Cove river. It was beyond my simple needs, and the whole thing was an embarrassment, to say nothing of the associations of the house with my dead mother, which exercised a painful and depressing effect on me. So I sold the house, and cut myself adrift. For a year or more I pursued the life of a lonely vagabond in New South Wales, painting as well as I could its scattered forests of magnificent trees, with their curious upturned foliage. Then, miserably dissatisfied with my performance, and altogether filled with a restless spirit, I determined to quit the colony and live in England, or at any rate somewhere in Europe. I would paint at the Paris schools, I promised myself, and acquire that technical mastery of my material that I now felt the lack of.

The thing was no sooner resolved on than begun. I instructed my solicitors in Sydney to wind up my affairs and to communicate with their London correspondents in order that, on my arrival in England, I might deal with business matters through them. I had more than half resolved to transfer all my property to England, and to make the old country my permanent headquarters; and in three weeks from the date of my resolve I had started. I carried with me the necessary letters of introduction to the London solicitors, and the deeds appertaining to certain land in South Australia, which my father had bought just before his departure on the fatal European trip. There was workable copper in this land, it had since been ascertained, and I believed I might profitably dispose of the property to a company in London.

I found myself to some extent out of my element on board a great passenger steamer. It seemed no longer possible for me in the constant association of shipboard to maintain that reserve which had become with me a second nature. But so much had it become my nature that I shrank ridiculously from breaking it, for, grown man as I was, it must be confessed that I was absurdly shy, and indeed I fear little better than an overgrown schoolboy in my manner. But somehow I was scarce a day at sea before falling into a most pleasant acquaintanceship with another passenger, a man of thirty-eight or forty, whose name was Dorrington. He was a tall, well-built fellow, rather handsome, perhaps, except for a certain extreme roundness of face and fulness of feature; he had a dark military moustache, and carried himself erect, with a swing as of a cavalryman, and his eyes had, I think, the most penetrating quality I ever saw. His manners were extremely engaging, and he was the only good talker I had ever met. He knew everybody, and had been everywhere. His fund of illustration and anecdote was inexhaustible, and during all my acquaintance with him I never heard him tell the same story twice. Nothing could happen—not a bird could fly by the ship, not a dish could be put on the table, but Dorrington was ready with a pungent remark and the appropriate anecdote. And he never bored nor wearied one. With all his ready talk he never appeared unduly obtrusive nor in the least egotistic. Mr. Horace Dorrington was altogether the most charming person I had ever met. Moreover we discovered a community of taste in cigars.

"By the way," said Dorrington to me one magnificent evening as we leaned on the rail and smoked, "Rigby isn't a very common name in Australia, is it? I seem to remember a case, twenty years ago or more, of an Australian gentleman of that name being very badly treated in London—indeed, now I think of it, I'm not sure that he wasn't murdered. Ever hear anything of it?"

"Yes," I said, "I heard a great deal, unfortunately. He was my father, and he *was* murdered."

"Your father? There—I'm awfully sorry. Perhaps I shouldn't have mentioned it; but of course I didn't know."

"Oh," I replied, "that's all right. It's so far back now that I don't mind speaking about it. It was a very extraordinary thing altogether." And then, feeling that I owed Dorrington a story of some sort, after listening to the many he had been telling me, I described to him the whole circumstances of my father's death.

"Ah," said Dorrington when I had finished, "I have heard of the Camorra before this—I know a thing or two about it, indeed. As a matter of fact it still exists; not quite the widespread and open thing it once was, of course, and much smaller; but pretty active in a quiet way, and pretty mischievous. They were a mighty bad lot, those Camorristi. Personally I'm rather surprised that you heard no more of them. They were the sort of people who would rather any day murder three people than one, and their usual idea of revenge went a good way beyond the mere murder of the offending party; they had a way of including his wife and family, and as many relatives as possible. But at any rate *you* seem to have got off all right, though I'm inclined to call it rather a piece of luck than otherwise."

Then, as was his invariable habit, he launched into anecdote. He told me of the crimes of the Maffia, that Italian secret society, larger even and more powerful than the Camorra, and almost as criminal; tales of implacable revenge visited on father, son, and grandson in succession, till the race was extirpated. Then he talked of the methods; of the large funds at the disposal of the Camorra and the Maffia, and of the cunning patience with which their schemes were carried into execution; of the victims who had discovered too late that their most trusted servants were sworn to their destruction, and of those who had fled to remote parts of the earth and hoped to be lost and forgotten, but who had been shadowed and slain with barbarous ferocity in their most trusted hiding-places. Wherever Italians were, there was apt to be a branch of one of the societies, and one could never tell where they might or might not turn up. The two Italian forecastle hands on board at that moment might be members, and might or might not have some business in hand not included in their signed articles.

I asked if he had ever come into personal contact with either of these societies or their doings.

"With the Camorra, no, though I know things about them that would probably surprise some of them not a little. But I have had professional dealings with the Maffia—and that without coming off second best, too. But it was not so serious a case as your father's; one of a robbery of documents and blackmail."

"Professional dealings?" I queried.

Dorrington laughed. "Yes," he answered. "I find I've come very near to letting the cat out of the bag. I don't generally tell people who I am when I travel about, and indeed I don't always use my own name, as I am doing now. Surely you've heard the name at some time or another?"

I had to confess that I did not remember it. But I excused myself by citing my secluded life, and the fact that I had never left Australia since I was a child.

"Ah," he said, "of course we should be less heard of in Australia. But in England we're really pretty well known, my partner and I. But, come now, look me all over and consider, and I'll give you a dozen guesses and bet you a sovereign you can't tell me my trade. And it's not such an uncommon or unheard-of trade, neither."

Guessing would have been hopeless, and I said so. He did not seem the sort of man who would trouble himself about a trade at all. I gave it up.

"Well," he said, "I've no particular desire to have it known all over the ship, but I don't mind telling you—you'd find it out probably before long if you settle in the old country—that we are what is called private inquiry agents—detectives—secret service men—whatever you like to call it."

"Indeed!"

"Yes, indeed. And I think I may claim that we stand as high as any— if not a trifle higher. Of course I can't tell you, but you'd be rather astonished if you heard the names of some of our clients. We have had dealings with certain royalties, European and Asiatic, that would startle you a bit if I could tell them. Dorrington & Hicks is the name of the firm, and we are both pretty busy men, though we keep going a regiment of assistants and correspondents. I have been in Australia three months over a rather awkward and complicated matter, but I fancy I've pulled it through pretty well, and I mean to reward myself with a little holiday when I get back. There—now you know the worst of me. And D. & H. present their respectful compliments, and trust that by unfailing punctuality and a strict attention to business they may hope to receive your esteemed commands whenever you may be so unfortunate as to require their services. Family secrets extracted, cleaned, scaled, or stopped with gold. Special attention given to wholesale orders." He laughed and pulled out his cigar-case. "You haven't another cigar in your pocket," he said, "or you wouldn't smoke that stump so low. Try one of these."

I took the cigar and lit it at my remainder. "Ah, then," I said, "I take it that it is the practice of your profession that has given you such a command of curious and out-of-the-way information and anecdote. Plainly you must have been in the midst of many curious affairs."

"Yes, I believe you," Dorrington replied. "But, as it happens, the most curious of my experiences I am unable to relate, since they are matters of professional confidence. Such as I *can* tell I usually tell with altered names, dates, and places. One learns discretion in such a trade as mine."

"As to your adventure with the Maffia, now. Is there any secrecy about that?"

Dorrington shrugged his shoulders. "No," he said, "none in particular. But the case was not particularly interesting. It was in Florence. The documents were the property of a wealthy American, and some of the Maffia rascals managed to steal them. It doesn't matter what the documents were—that's a private matter—but their owner would have parted with a great deal to get them back, and the Maffia held them for ransom. But they had such a fearful notion of the American's wealth, and of what he ought to pay, that, badly as he wanted the papers back, he couldn't stand their demands, and employed us to negotiate and to do our best for him. I think I might have managed to get the things stolen back again—indeed I spent some time thinking a plan over—but I decided in the end that it wouldn't pay. If the Maffia were tricked in that way they might consider it appropriate to stick somebody with a knife, and that was not an easy thing to provide against. So I took a little time and went another way to work. The details don't matter— they're quite uninteresting, and to tell you them would be to talk mere professional 'shop'; there's a deal of dull and patient work to be done in my business. Anyhow, I contrived to find out exactly in whose hands the documents lay. He wasn't altogether a blameless creature, and there were two or three little things that, properly handled, might have brought him into awkward complications with the law. So I delayed the negotiations while I got my nets effectually round this gentleman, who was the president of that particular branch of the Maffia, and when all was ready I had a friendly interview with him, and just showed him my hand of cards. They served as no other argument would have done, and in the end we concluded quite an amicable arrangement on easy terms for both parties, and my client got his property back, including all expenses, at about a fifth of the price he expected to have to pay. That's all. I learnt a deal about the Maffia while the business lasted, and at that and other times I learnt a good deal about the Camorra too."

Dorrington and I grew more intimate every day of the voyage, till he knew every detail of my uneventful little history, and I knew many of his own most curious experiences. In truth he was a man with an irresistible fascination for a dull home-bird like myself. With all his gaiety he never forgot business, and at most of our stopping places he sent off messages by cable to his partner. As the voyage drew near its end he grew anxious and impatient lest he should not arrive in time to enable him to get to Scotland for grouse-shooting on the twelfth of August. His one amusement, it seemed, was shooting, and the holiday he had promised himself was to be spent on a grouse-moor which he rented in Perthshire. It would be a great nuisance to miss the twelfth, he said, but it would apparently be a near shave. He thought, however, that in any case it might be done by leaving the ship at Plymouth, and rushing up to London by the first train.

"Yes," he said, "I think I shall be able to do it that way, even if the boat is a couple of days late. By the way," he added suddenly, "why not come along to Scotland with me? You haven't any particular business in hand, and I can promise you a week or two of good fun."

The invitation pleased me. "It's very good of you," I said, "and as a matter of fact I haven't any very urgent business in London. I must see those solicitors I told you of, but that's not a matter of hurry; indeed an hour or two on my way through London would be enough. But as I don't know any of your party and—"

"Pooh, pooh, my dear fellow," answered Dorrington, with a snap of his fingers, "that's all right. I shan't have a party. There won't be time to get it together. One or two might come down a little later, but if they do they'll be capital fellows, delighted to make your acquaintance, I'm sure. Indeed you'll do me a great favour if you'll come, else I shall be all alone, without a soul to say a word to. Anyway, I *won't* miss the twelfth, if it's to be done by any possibility. You'll really have to come, you know— you've no excuse. I can lend you guns and anything you want, though I believe you've such things with you. Who is your London solicitor, by the way?"

"Mowbray, of Lincoln's Inn Fields."

"Oh, Mowbray? We know him well; his partner died last year. When I say *we* know him well, I mean as a firm. I have never met him personally, though my partner (who does the office work) has regular dealings with him. He's an excellent man, but his managing clerk's frightful; I wonder Mowbray keeps him. Don't you let him do anything for you on his own hook; he makes the most disastrous messes, and I rather fancy he drinks. Deal with Mowbray himself; there's nobody better in London. And by the way, now I think of it, it's lucky you've nothing urgent for him, for he's sure to be off out of town for the twelfth; he's a rare old gunner, and never misses a season. So that now you haven't a shade of an excuse for leaving me in the lurch, and we'll consider the thing settled."

Settled accordingly it was, and the voyage ended uneventfully. But the steamer was late, and we left it at Plymouth and rushed up to town on the tenth. We had three or four hours to prepare before leaving Euston by the night train. Dorrington's moor was a long drive from Crieff station, and he calculated that at best we could not arrive there before the early evening of the following day, which would, however, give us comfortable time for a good long night's rest before the morning's sport opened. Fortunately I had plenty of loose cash with me, so that there was nothing to delay us in that regard. We made ready in Dorrington's rooms (he was a bachelor) in Conduit Street, and got off comfortably by the ten o'clock train from Euston.

Then followed a most delightful eight days. The weather was fine, the birds were plentiful, and my first taste of grouse-shooting was a complete success. I resolved for the future to come out of my shell and mix in the world that contained such charming fellows as Dorrington, and such delightful sports as that I was then enjoying. But on the eighth day Dorrington received a telegram calling him instantly to London.

"It's a shocking nuisance," he said; "here's my holiday either knocked on the head altogether or cut in two, and I fear it's the first rather than the second. It's just the way in such an uncertain profession as mine. There's no possible help for it, however; I must go, as you'd understand at once if you knew the case. But what chiefly annoys me is leaving you all alone."

I reassured him on this point, and pointed out that I had for a long time been used to a good deal of my own company. Though indeed, with Dorrington away, life at the shooting-lodge threatened to be less pleasant than it had been.

"But you'll be bored to death here," Dorrington said, his thoughts jumping with my own. "But on the other hand it won't be much good going up to town yet. Everybody's out of town, and Mowbray among them. There's a little business of ours that's waiting for him at this moment—my partner mentioned it in his letter yesterday. Why not put in the time with a little tour round? Or you might work up to London by irregular stages, and look about you. As an artist you'd like to see a few of the old towns—probably, Edinburgh, Chester, Warwick, and so on. It isn't a great programme, perhaps, but I hardly know what else to suggest. As for myself I must be off as I am by the first train I can get."

I begged him not to trouble about me, but to attend to his business. As a matter of fact, I was disposed to get to London and take chambers, at any rate for a little while. But Chester was a place I much wanted to see—a real old town, with walls round it—and I was not indisposed to take a day at Warwick. So in the end I resolved to pack up and make for Chester the following day, and from there to take train for Warwick. And in half an hour Dorrington was gone.

Chester was all delight to me. My recollections of the trip to Europe in my childhood were vivid enough as to the misfortunes that followed my father, but of the ancient buildings we visited I remembered little. Now in Chester I found the mediæval town I had so often read of. I wandered for hours together in the quaint old "Rows," and walked on the city wall. The evening after my arrival was fine and moonlight, and I was tempted from my hotel. I took a stroll about the town and finished by a walk along the wall from the Watergate toward the cathedral. The moon, flecked over now and again by scraps of cloud, and at times obscured for half a minute together, lighted up all the Roodee in the intervals, and touched with silver the river beyond. But as I walked I presently grew aware of a quiet shuffling footstep some little way behind me. I took little heed of it at first, though I could see nobody near me from whom the sound might come. But soon I perceived that when I stopped, as I did from time to time to gaze over the parapet, the mysterious footsteps stopped also, and when I resumed my walk the quiet shuffling tread began again. At first I thought it might be an echo; but a moment's reflection dispelled that idea. Mine was an even, distinct walk, and this which followed was a soft, quick, shuffling step—a mere scuffle. Moreover, when, by way of test, I took a few silent steps on tip-toe, the shuffle still persisted. I was being followed.

Now I do not know whether or not it may sound like a childish fancy, but I confess I thought of my father. When last I had been in England, as a child, my father's violent death had been preceded by just such followings. And now after all these years, on my return, on the very first night I walked abroad alone, there were strange footsteps in my track. The walk was narrow, and nobody could possibly pass me unseen. I turned suddenly, therefore, and hastened back. At once I saw a dark figure rise from the shadow of the parapet and run. I ran too, but I could not gain on the figure, which receded farther and more indistinctly before me. One reason was that I felt doubtful of my footing on the unfamiliar track. I ceased my chase, and continued my stroll. It might easily have been some vagrant thief, I thought, who had a notion to rush, at a convenient opportunity, and snatch my watch. But here I was far past the spot where I had turned there was the shuffling footstep behind me again. For a little while I feigned not to notice it; then, swinging round as swiftly as I could, I made a quick rush. Useless again, for there in the distance scuttled that same indistinct figure, more rapidly than I could run. What did it mean? I liked the affair so little that I left the walls and walked toward my hotel.

The streets were quiet. I had traversed two, and was about emerging into one of the two main streets, where the Rows are, when, from the farther part of the dark street behind me, there came once more the sound of the now unmistakable footstep. I stopped; the footsteps stopped also. I turned and walked back a few steps, and as I did it the sounds went scuffling away at the far end of the street.

It could not be fancy. It could not be chance. For a single incident perhaps such an explanation might serve, but not for this persistent recurrence. I hurried away to my hotel, resolved, since I could not come at my pursuer, to turn back no more. But before I reached the hotel there were the shuffling footsteps again, and not far behind.

It would not be true to say that I was alarmed at this stage of the adventure, but I was troubled to know what it all might mean, and altogether puzzled to account for it. I thought a great deal, but I went to bed and rose in the morning no wiser than ever.

Whether or not it was a mere fancy induced by the last night's experience I cannot say, but I went about that day with a haunting feeling that I was watched, and to me the impression was very real indeed. I listened often, but in the bustle of the day, even in quiet old Chester, the individual characters of different footsteps were not easily recognisable. Once, however, as I descended a flight of steps from the Rows, I fancied I heard the quick shuffle in the curious old gallery I had just quitted. I turned up the steps again and looked. There was a shabby sort of man looking in one of the windows, and leaning so far as to hide his head behind the heavy oaken pilaster that supported the building above. It might have been his footstep, or it might have been my fancy. At any rate I would have a look at him. I mounted the top stair, but as I turned in his direction the man ran off, with his face averted and his head ducked, and vanished down another stair. I made all speed after him, but when I reached the street he was nowhere to be seen.

What *could* it all mean? The man was rather above the middle height, and he wore one of those soft felt hats familiar on the head of the London organ-grinder. Also his hair was black and bushy, and protruded over the back of his coat-collar. Surely *this* was no delusion; surely I was not imagining an Italian aspect for this man simply because of the recollection of my father's fate?

Perhaps I was foolish, but I took no more pleasure in Chester. The embarrassment was a novel one for me, and I could not forget it. I went back to my hotel, paid my bill, sent my bag to the railway station, and took train for Warwick by way of Crewe.

It was dark when I arrived, but the night was near as fine as last night had been at Chester. I took a very little late dinner at my hotel, and fell into a doubt what to do with myself. One rather fat and very sleepy commercial traveller was the only other customer visible, and the billiard room was empty. There seemed to be nothing to do but to light a cigar and take a walk.

I could just see enough of the old town to give me good hopes of to-morrow's sight-seeing. There was nothing visible of quite such an interesting character as one might meet in Chester, but there were a good few fine old sixteenth century houses, and there were the two gates with the chapels above them. But of course the castle was the great show-place, and that I should visit on the morrow, if there were no difficulties as to permission. There were some very fine pictures there, if I remembered aright what I had read. I was walking down the incline from one of the gates, trying to remember who the painters of these pictures were, besides Van Dyck and Holbein, when—that shuffling step was behind me again!

I admit that it cost me an effort, this time, to turn on my pursuer. There was something uncanny in that persistent, elusive footstep, and indeed there was something alarming in my circumstances, dogged thus from place to place, and unable to shake off my enemy, or to understand his movements or his motive. Turn I did, however, and straightway the shuffling step went off at a hastened pace in the shadow of the gate. This time I made no more than half-a-dozen steps back. I turned again, and pushed my way to the hotel. And as I went the shuffling step came after.

The thing was serious. There must be some object in this unceasing watching, and the object could bode no good to me. Plainly some unseen eye had been on me the whole of that day, had noted my goings and comings and my journey from Chester. Again, and irresistibly, the watchings that preceded my father's death came to mind, and I could not forget them. I could have no doubt now that I had been closely watched from the moment I had set foot at Plymouth. But who could have been waiting to watch me at Plymouth, when indeed I had only decided to land at the last moment? Then I thought of the two Italian forecastle hands on the steamer—the very men whom Dorrington had used to illustrate in what unexpected quarters members of the terrible Italian secret societies might be found. And the Camorra was not satisfied with single revenge; it destroyed the son after the father, and it waited for many years, with infinite patience and cunning.

Dogged by the steps, I reached the hotel and went to bed. I slept but fitfully at first, though better rest came as the night wore on. In the early morning I woke with a sudden shock, and with an indefinite sense of being disturbed by somebody about me. The window was directly opposite the foot of the bed, and there, as I looked, was the face of a man, dark, evil, and grinning, with a bush of black hair about his uncovered head, and small rings in his ears.

It was but a flash, and the face vanished. I was struck by the terror that one so often feels on a sudden and violent awakening from sleep, and it was some seconds ere I could leave my bed and get to the window. My room was on the first floor, and the window looked down on a stable-yard. I had a momentary glimpse of a human figure leaving the gate of the yard, and it was the figure that had fled before me in the Rows, at Chester. A ladder belonging to the yard stood under the window, and that was all.

I rose and dressed; I could stand this sort of thing no longer. If it were only something tangible, if there were only somebody I could take hold of, and fight with if necessary, it would not have been so bad. But I was surrounded by some mysterious machination, persistent, unexplainable, that it was altogether impossible to tackle or to face. To complain to the police would have been absurd—they would take me for a lunatic. They are indeed just such complaints that lunatics so often make to the police—complaints of being followed by indefinite enemies, and of being besieged by faces that look in at windows. Even if they did not set me down a lunatic, what could the police of a provincial town do for me in a case like this? No, I must go and consult Dorrington.

I had my breakfast, and then decided that I would at any rate try the castle before leaving. Try it I did accordingly, and was allowed to go over it. But through the whole morning I was oppressed by the horrible sense of being watched by malignant eyes. Clearly there was no comfort for me while this lasted; so after lunch I caught a train which brought me to Euston soon after half-past six.

I took a cab straight to Dorrington's rooms, but he was out, and was not expected home till late. So I drove to a large hotel near Charing Cross—I avoid mentioning its name for reasons which will presently be understood—sent in my bag, and dined.

I had not the smallest doubt but that I was still under the observation of the man or the men who had so far pursued me; I had, indeed, no hope of eluding them, except by the contrivance of Dorrington's expert brain. So as I had no desire to hear that shuffling footstep again—indeed it had seemed, at Warwick, to have a physically painful effect on my nerves—I stayed within and got to bed early.

I had no fear of waking face to face with a grinning Italian here. My window was four floors up, out of reach of anything but a fire-escape. And, in fact, I woke comfortably and naturally, and saw nothing from my window but the bright sky, the buildings opposite, and the traffic below. But as I turned to close my door behind me as I emerged into the corridor, there, on the muntin of the frame, just below the bedroom number, was a little round paper label, perhaps a trifle smaller than a sixpence, and on the label, drawn awkwardly in ink, was a device of two crossed knives of curious, crooked shape. The sign of the Camorra!

I will not attempt to describe the effect of this sign upon me. It may best be imagined, in view of what I have said of the incidents preceding the murder of my father. It was the sign of an inexorable fate, creeping nearer step by step, implacable, inevitable, and mysterious. In little more than twelve hours after seeing that sign my father had been a mangled corpse. One of the hotel servants passed as I stood by the door, and I made shift to ask him if he knew anything of the label. He looked at the paper, and then, more curiously, at me, but he could offer no explanation. I spent little time over breakfast, and then went by cab to Conduit Street. I paid my bill and took my bag with me.

Dorrington had gone to his office, but he had left a message that if I called I was to follow him; and the office was in Bedford Street, Covent Garden. I turned the cab in that direction forthwith.

ARTHUR MORRISON

"Why," said Dorrington as we shook hands, "I believe you look a bit out of sorts! Doesn't England agree with you?"

"Well," I answered, "it has proved rather trying so far." And then I described, in exact detail, my adventures as I have set them down here.

Dorrington looked grave. "It's really extraordinary," he said, "most extraordinary; and it isn't often that I call a thing extraordinary neither, with my experience. But it's plain something must be done—something to gain time at any rate. We're in the dark at present, of course, and I expect I shall have to fish about a little before I get at anything to go on. In the meantime I think you must disappear as artfully as we can manage it." He sat silent for a little while, thoughtfully tapping his forehead with his finger-tips. "I wonder," he said presently, "whether or not those Italian fellows on the steamer *are* in it or not. I suppose you haven't made yourself known anywhere, have you?"

"Nowhere. As you know, you've been with me all the time till you left the moor, and since then I have been with nobody and called on nobody."

"Now there's no doubt it's the Camorra," Dorrington said—"that's pretty plain. I think I told you on the steamer that it was rather wonderful that you had heard nothing of them after your father's death. What has caused them all this delay there's no telling—they know best themselves; it's been lucky for you, anyway, so far. What I'd like to find out now is how they have identified you, and got on your track so promptly. There's no guessing where these fellows get their information—it's just wonderful; but if we can find out, then perhaps we can stop the supply, or turn on something that will lead them into a pit. If you had called anywhere on business and declared yourself—as you might have done, for instance, at Mowbray's—I might be inclined to suspect that they got the tip in some crooked way from there. But you haven't. Of course, if those Italian chaps on the steamer *are* in it, you're probably identified pretty certainly; but if they're not, they may only have made a guess. We two landed together, and kept together, till a day or two ago; as far as any outsider would know, I might be Rigby and you might be Dorrington. Come, we'll work on those lines. I think I smell a plan. Are you staying anywhere?"

"No. I paid my bill at the hotel and came along here with my bag."

"Very well. Now there's a house at Highgate kept by a very trustworthy man, whom I know very well, where a man might be pretty comfortable for a few days, or even for a week, if he doesn't mind staying indoors, and keeping himself out of sight. I expect your friends of the Camorra are watching in the street outside at this moment; but I think it will be fairly easy to get you away to Highgate without letting them into the secret, if you don't mind secluding yourself for a bit. In the circumstances, I take it you won't object at all?"

"Object? I should think not."

"Very well, that's settled. You can call yourself Dorrington or not, as you please, though perhaps it will be safest not to shout 'Rigby' too loud. But as for myself, for a day or two at least I'm going to be Mr. James Rigby. Have you your card-case handy?"

"Yes, here it is. But then, as to taking my name, won't you run serious risk?"

Dorrington winked merrily. "I've run a risk or two before now," he said, "in course of my business. And if *I* don't mind the risk, you needn't grumble, for I warn you I shall charge for risk when I send you my bill. And I think I can take care of myself fairly well, even with the Camorra about. I shall take you to this place at Highgate, and then you won't see me for a few days. It won't do for me, in the character of Mr. James Rigby, to go dragging a trail up and down between this place and your retreat. You've got some other identifying papers, haven't you?"

"Yes, I have." I produced the letter from my Sydney lawyers to Mowbray, and the deeds of the South Australian property from my bag.

"Ah," said Dorrington, "I'll just give you a formal receipt for these, since they're valuable; it's a matter of business, and we'll do it in a business-like way. I may want something solid like this to support any bluff I may have to make. A mere case of cards won't always act, you know. It's a pity old Mowbray's out of town, for there's a way in which he might give a little help, I fancy. But never mind—leave it all to me. There's your receipt. Keep it snug away somewhere, where inquisitive people can't read it."

He handed me the receipt, and then took me to his partner's room and introduced me. Mr. Hicks was a small, wrinkled man, older than Dorrington, I should think, by fifteen or twenty years, and with all the aspect and manner of a quiet old professional man.

Dorrington left the room, and presently returned with his hat in his hand. "Yes," he said, "there's a charming dark gentleman with a head like a mop, and rings in his ears, skulking about at the next corner. If it was he who looked in at your window, I don't wonder you were startled. His dress suggests the organ-grinding interest, but he looks as though cutting a throat would be more in his line than grinding a tune; and no doubt he has friends as engaging as himself close at call. If you'll come with me now I think we shall give him the slip. I have a growler ready for you—a hansom's a bit too glassy and public. Pull down the blinds and sit back when you get inside."

He led me to a yard at the back of the building wherein the office stood, from which a short flight of steps led to a basement. We followed a passage in this basement till we reached another flight, and ascending these, we emerged into the corridor of another building. Out at the door at the end of this, and we passed a large block of model dwellings, and were in Bedfordbury. Here a four-wheeler was waiting, and I shut myself in it without delay.

I was to proceed as far as King's Cross in this cab, Dorrington had arranged, and there he would overtake me in a swift hansom. It fell out as he had settled, and, dismissing the hansom, he came the rest of the journey with me in the four-wheeler.

We stopped at length before one of a row of houses, apparently recently built—houses of the over-ornamented, gabled and tiled sort that abound in the suburbs.

"Crofting is the man's name," Dorrington said, as we alighted. "He's rather an odd sort of customer, but quite decent in the main, and his wife makes coffee such as money won't buy in most places."

A woman answered Dorrington's ring—a woman of most extreme thinness. Dorrington greeted her as Mrs. Crofting, and we entered.

"We've just lost our servant again, Mr. Dorrington," the woman said in a shrill voice, "and Mr. Crofting ain't at home. But I'm expecting him before long."

"I don't think I need wait to see him, Mrs. Crofting," Dorrington answered. "I'm sure I can't leave my friend in better hands than yours. I hope you've a vacant room?"

"Well, for a friend of yours, Mr. Dorrington, no doubt we can find room."

"That's right. My friend Mr."—Dorrington gave me a meaning look—"Mr. Phelps, would like to stay here for a few days. He wants to be quite quiet for a little—do you understand?"

"Oh, yes, Mr. Dorrington, I understand."

"Very well, then, make him as comfortable as you can, and give him some of your very best coffee. I believe you've got quite a little library of books, and Mr. Phelps will be glad of them. Have you got any cigars?" Dorrington added, turning to me.

"Yes; there are some in my bag."

"Then I think you'll be pretty comfortable now. Goodbye. I expect you'll see me in a few days—or at any rate you'll get a message. Meantime be as happy as you can."

Dorrington left, and the woman showed me to a room upstairs, where I placed my bag. In front, on the same floor, was a sitting-room, with, I suppose, some two or three hundred books, mostly novels, on shelves. The furniture of the place was of the sort one expects to find in an ordinary lodging-house—horsehair sofas, loo tables, lustres, and so forth. Mrs. Crofting explained to me that the customary dinner hour was two, but that I might dine when I liked. I elected, however, to follow the custom of the house, and sat down to a cigar and a book.

At two o'clock the dinner came, and I was agreeably surprised to find it a very good one, much above what the appointments of the house had led me to expect. Plainly Mrs. Crofting was a capital cook. There was no soup, but there was a very excellent sole, and some well-done cutlets with peas, and an omelet; also a bottle of Bass. Come, I felt that I should not do so badly in this place after all. I trusted that Dorrington would be as comfortable in his half of the transaction, bearing my responsibilities and troubles. I had heard a heavy, blundering tread on the floor below, and judged from this that Mr. Crofting had returned.

After dinner I lit a cigar, and Mrs. Crofting brought her coffee. Truly it was excellent coffee, and brewed as I like it—strong and black, and plenty of it. It had a flavour of its own too, novel, but not unpleasing. I took one cupful, and brought another to my side as I lay on the sofa with my book. I had not read six lines before I was asleep.

I woke with a sensation of numbing cold in my right side, a terrible stiffness in my limbs, and a sound of loud splashing in my ears. All was pitch dark, and—what was this? Water! Water all about me. I was lying in six inches of cold water, and more was pouring down upon me from above. My head was afflicted with a splitting ache. But where was I? Why was it dark? And whence all the water? I staggered to my feet, and instantly struck my head against a hard roof above me. I raised my hand; there was the roof or whatever place it was, hard, smooth and cold, and little more than five feet from the floor, so that I bent as I stood. I spread my hand to the side; that was hard, smooth and cold too. And then the conviction struck me like a blow—I was in a covered iron tank, and the water was pouring in to drown me!

I dashed my hands frantically against the lid, and strove to raise it. It would not move. I shouted at the top of my voice, and turned about to feel the extent of my prison. One way I could touch the opposite sides at once easily with my hands, the other way it was wider—perhaps a little more than six feet altogether. What was this? Was this to be my fearful end, cooped in this tank while the water rose by inches to choke me? Already the water was a foot deep. I flung myself at the sides, I beat the pitiless iron with fists, face and head, I screamed and implored. Then it struck me that I might at least stop the inlet of water. I put out my hand and felt the falling stream, then found the inlet and stopped it with my fingers. But water still poured in with a resounding splash; there was another opening at the opposite end, which I could not reach without releasing the one I now held! I was but prolonging my agony. Oh, the devilish cunning that had devised those two inlets, so far apart! Again I beat the sides, broke my nails with tearing at the corners, screamed and entreated in my agony. I was mad, but with no dulling of the senses, for the horrors of my awful, helpless state, overwhelmed my brain, keen and perceptive to every ripple of the unceasing water.

In the height of my frenzy I held my breath, for I heard a sound from outside. I shouted again—implored some quicker death. Then there was a scraping on the lid above me, and it was raised at one edge, and let in the light of a candle. I sprang from my knees and forced the lid back, and the candle flame danced before me. The candle was held by a dusty man, a workman apparently, who stared at me with scared eyes, and said nothing but, "Goo' lor'!"

Overhead were the rafters of a gabled roof, and tilted against them was the thick beam which, jammed across from one sloping rafter to another, had held the tank-lid fast. "Help me!" I gasped. "Help me out!"

The man took me by the armpits and hauled me, dripping and half dead, over the edge of the tank, into which the water still poured, making a noise in the hollow iron that half drowned our voices. The man had been at work on the cistern of a neighbouring house, and hearing an uncommon noise, he had climbed through the spaces left in the party walls to give passage along under the roofs to the builders' men. Among the joists at our feet was the trap-door through which, drugged and insensible, I had been carried, to be flung into that horrible cistern.

With the help of my friend the workman I made shift to climb through by the way he had come. We got back to the house where he had been at work, and there the people gave me brandy and lent me dry clothes. I made haste to send for the police, but when they arrived Mrs. Crofting and her respectable spouse had gone. Some unusual noise in the roof must have warned them. And when the police, following my directions further, got to the offices of Dorrington and Hicks, those acute professional men had gone too, but in such haste that the contents of the office, papers and everything else, had been left just as they stood.

The plot was clear now. The followings, the footsteps, the face at the window, the label on the door—all were a mere humbug arranged by Dorrington for his own purpose, which was to drive me into his power and get my papers from me. Armed with these, and with his consummate address and knowledge of affairs, he could go to Mr. Mowbray in the character of Mr. James Rigby, sell my land in South Australia, and have the whole of my property transferred to himself from Sydney. The rest of my baggage was at his rooms; if any further proof were required it might be found there. He had taken good care that I should not meet Mr. Mowbray—who, by the way, I afterwards found had not left his office, and had never fired a gun in his life. At first I wondered that Dorrington had not made some murderous attempt on me at the shooting place in Scotland. But a little thought convinced me that that would have been bad policy for him. The disposal of the body would be difficult, and he would have to account somehow for my sudden disappearance. Whereas, by the use of his Italian assistant and his murder apparatus at Highgate I was made to efface my own trail, and could be got rid of in the end with little trouble; for my body, stripped of everything that might identify me, would be simply that of a drowned man unknown, whom nobody could identify. The whole plot was contrived upon the information I myself had afforded Dorrington during the voyage home. And it all sprang from his remembering the report of my father's death. When the papers in the office came to be examined, there each step in the operations was plainly revealed. There was a code telegram from Suez directing Hicks to hire a grouse moor. There were telegrams and letters from Scotland giving directions as to the later movements; indeed the thing was displayed completely. The business of Dorrington and Hicks had really been that of private inquiry agents, and they had done much *bonâ fide* business; but many of their operations had been of a more than questionable sort. And among their papers were found complete sets, neatly arranged in dockets, each containing in skeleton a complete history of a case. Many of these cases were of a most interesting character, and I have been enabled to piece together, out of the material thus supplied, the narratives which will follow this. As to my own case, it only remains to say that as yet neither Dorrington, Hicks, nor the Croftings have been caught. They played in the end for a high stake (they might have made six figures of me if they had killed me, and the first figure would not have been a one) and they lost by a mere accident. But I have often wondered how many of the bodies which the coroners' juries of London have returned to be "Found Drowned" were drowned, not where they were picked up, but in that horrible tank at Highgate. What the drug was that gave Mrs. Crofting's coffee its value in Dorrington's eyes I do not know, but plainly it had not been sufficient in my case to keep me unconscious against the shock of cold water till I could be drowned altogether. Months have passed since my adventure, but even now I sweat at the sight of an iron tank.

II

The Case of Janissary

I

In this case (and indeed in most of the others) the notes and other documents found in the dockets would, by themselves, give but a faint outline of the facts, and, indeed, might easily be unintelligible to many people, especially as for much of my information I have been indebted to outside inquiries. Therefore I offer no excuse for presenting the whole thing digested into plain narrative form, with little reference to my authorities. Though I knew none of the actors in it, with the exception of the astute Dorrington, the case was especially interesting to me, as will be gathered from the narrative itself.

The only paper in the bundle which I shall particularly allude to was a newspaper cutting, of a date anterior by nine or ten months to the events I am to write of. It had evidently been cut at the time it appeared, and saved, in case it might be useful, in a box in the form of a book, containing many hundreds of others. From this receptacle it had been taken, and attached to the bundle during the progress of the case. I may say at once that the facts recorded had no direct concern with the case of the horse Janissary, but had been useful in affording a suggestion to Dorrington in connection therewith. The matter is the short report of an ordinary sort of inquest, and I here transcribe it.

"Dr. McCulloch held an inquest yesterday on the body of Mr. Henry Lawrence, whose body was found on Tuesday morning last in the river near Vauxhall Bridge. The deceased was well known in certain sporting circles. Sophia Lawrence, the widow, said that deceased had left home on Monday afternoon at about five, in his usual health, saying that he was to dine at a friend's, and she saw nothing more of him till called upon to identify the body. He had no reason for suicide, and so far as witness knew, was free from pecuniary embarrassments. He had, indeed, been very successful in betting recently. He habitually carried a large pocket-book, with papers in it. Mr. Robert Naylor, commission agent, said that deceased dined with him that evening at his house in Gold Street, Chelsea, and left for home at about half-past eleven. He had at the time a sum of nearly four hundred pounds upon him, chiefly in notes, which had been paid him by witness in settlement of a bet. It was a fine night, and deceased walked in the direction of Chelsea Embankment. That was the last witness saw of him. He might not have been perfectly sober, but he was not drunk, and was capable of taking care of himself. The evidence of the Thames police went to show that no money was on the body when found, except a few coppers, and no pocket-book. Dr. William Hodgetts said that death was due to drowning. There were some bruises on the arms and head which might have been caused before death. The body was a very healthy one. The coroner said that there seemed to be a very strong suspicion of foul play, unless the pocket-book of the deceased had got out of his pocket in the water; but the evidence was very meagre, although the police appeared to have made every possible inquiry. The jury returned a verdict of 'Found Drowned, though how the deceased came into the water there was no evidence to show.'"

I know no more of the unfortunate man Lawrence than this, and I have only printed the cutting here because it probably induced Dorrington to take certain steps in the case I am dealing with. With that case the fate of the man Lawrence has nothing whatever to do. He passes out of the story entirely.

II

Mr. Warren Telfer was a gentleman of means, and the owner of a few—very few—racehorses. But he had a great knack of buying hidden prizes in yearlings, and what his stable lacked in quantity it often more than made up for in quality. Thus he had once bought a St. Leger winner for as little as a hundred and fifty pounds. Many will remember his bitter disappointment of ten or a dozen years back, when his horse, Matfelon, starting an odds-on favourite for the Two Thousand, never even got among the crowd, and ambled in streets behind everything. It was freely rumoured (and no doubt with cause) that Matfelon had been "got at" and in some way "nobbled." There were hints of a certain bucket of water administered just before the race—a bucket of water observed in the hands, some said of one, some said of another person connected with Ritter's training establishment. There was no suspicion of pulling, for plainly the jockey was doing his best with the animal all the way along, and never had a tight rein. So a nobbling it must have been, said the knowing ones, and Mr. Warren Telfer said so too, with much bitterness. More, he immediately removed his horses from Ritter's stables, and started a small training place of his own for his own horses merely; putting an old steeplechase jockey in charge, who had come out of a bad accident permanently lame, and had fallen on evil days.

The owner was an impulsive and violent-tempered man, who, once a notion was in his head, held to it through everything, and in spite of everything. His misfortune with Matfelon made him the most insanely distrustful man alive. In everything he fancied he saw a trick, and to him every man seemed a scoundrel. He could scarce bear to let the very stable-boys touch his horses, and although for years all went as well as could be expected in his stables, his suspicious distrust lost nothing of its virulence. He was perpetually fussing about the stables, making surprise visits, and laying futile traps that convicted nobody. The sole tangible result of this behaviour was a violent quarrel between Mr. Warren Telfer and his nephew Richard, who had been making a lengthened stay with his uncle. Young Telfer, to tell the truth, was neither so discreet nor so exemplary in behaviour as he might have been, but his temper was that characteristic of the family, and when he conceived that his uncle had an idea that he was communicating stable secrets to friends outside, there was an animated row, and the nephew betook himself and his luggage somewhere else. Young Telfer always insisted, however, that his uncle was not a bad fellow on the whole, though he had habits of thought and conduct that made him altogether intolerable at times. But the uncle had no good word for his graceless nephew; and indeed Richard Telfer betted more than he could afford, and was not so particular in his choice of sporting acquaintances as a gentleman should have been.

Mr. Warren Telfer's house, "Blackhall," and his stables were little more than two miles from Redbury, in Hampshire; and after the quarrel Mr. Richard Telfer was not seen near the place for many months—not, indeed, till excitement was high over the forthcoming race for the Redbury Stakes, for which there was an entry from the stable—Janissary, for long ranked second favourite; and then the owner's nephew did not enter the premises, and, in fact, made his visit as secret as possible.

I have said that Janissary was long ranked second favourite for the Redbury Stakes, but a little more than a week before the race he became first favourite, owing to a training mishap to the horse fancied first, which made its chances so poor that it might have been scratched at any moment. And so far was Janissary above the class of the field (though it was a two-year-old race, and there might be a surprise) that it at once went to far shorter odds than the previous favourite, which, indeed, had it run fit and well, would have found Janissary no easy colt to beat.

Mr. Telfer's nephew was seen near the stables but two or three days before the race, and that day the owner despatched a telegram to the firm of Dorrington & Hicks. In response to this telegram, Dorrington caught the first available train for Redbury, and was with Mr. Warren Telfer in his library by five in the afternoon.

"It is about my horse Janissary that I want to consult you, Mr. Dorrington," said Mr. Telfer. "It's right enough now—or at least was right at exercise this morning—but I feel certain that there's some diabolical plot on hand somewhere to interfere with the horse before the Redbury Stakes day, and I'm sorry to have to say that I suspect my own nephew to be mixed up in it in some way. In the first place I may tell you that there is no doubt whatever that the colt, if let alone, and bar accident, can win in a canter. He could have won even if Herald, the late favourite, had kept well, for I can tell you that Janissary is a far greater horse than anybody is aware of outside my establishment—or at any rate, than anybody ought to be aware of, if the stable secrets are properly kept. His pedigree is nothing very great, and he never showed his quality till quite lately, in private trials. Of course it has leaked out somehow that the colt is exceptionally good—I don't believe I can trust a soul in the place. How should the price have gone up to five to four unless somebody had been telling what he's paid not to tell? But that isn't all, as I have said. I've a conviction that something's on foot—somebody wants to interfere with the horse. Of course we get a tout about now and again, but the downs are pretty big, and we generally manage to dodge them if we want to. On the last three or four mornings, however, wherever Janissary might be taking his gallop, there was a big, hulking fellow, with a red beard and spectacles—not so much watching the horse as trying to get hold of the lad. I am always up and out at five, for I've found to my cost—you remember about Matfelon—that if a man doesn't want to be ramped he must never take his eye off things. Well, I have scarcely seen the lad ease the colt once on the last three or four mornings without that red-bearded fellow bobbing up from a knoll, or a clump of bushes, or something, close by—especially if Janissary was a bit away from the other horses, and not under my nose, or the head lad's, for a moment. I rode at the fellow, of course, when I saw what he was after, but he was artful as a cartload of monkeys, and vanished somehow before I could get near him. The head lad believes he has seen him about just after dark, too; but I am keeping the stable lads in when they're not riding, and I suppose he finds he has no chance of getting at them except when they're out with the horses. This morning, not only did I see this fellow about, as usual, but, I am ashamed to say, I observed my own nephew acting the part of a common tout. He certainly had the decency to avoid me and clear out, but that was not all, as you shall see. This morning, happening to approach the stables from the back, I suddenly came upon the red-bearded man—giving money to a groom of mine! He ran off at once, as you may guess, and I discharged the groom where he stood, and would not allow him into the stables again. He offered no explanation or excuse, but took himself off, and half an hour afterward I almost sent away my head boy too. For when I told him of the dismissal, he admitted that he had seen that same groom taking money of my nephew at the back of the stables, an hour before, and had not informed me! He said that he thought that as it was 'only Mr. Richard' it didn't matter. Fool! Anyway, the groom has gone, and, so far as I can tell as yet, the colt is all right. I examined him at once, of course; and I also turned over a box that Weeks, the groom, used to keep brushes and odd things in. There I found this paper full of powder. I don't yet know what it is, but it's certainly nothing he had any business with in the stable. Will you take it?

"And now," Mr. Telfer went on, "I'm in such an uneasy state that I want your advice and assistance. Quite apart from the suspicious—more than suspicious—circumstances I have informed you of, I am *certain*—I know it without being able to give precise reasons—I am *certain* that some attempt is being made at disabling Janissary before Thursday's race. I feel it in my bones, so to speak. I had the same suspicion just before that Two Thousand, when Matfelon was got at. The thing was in the air, as it is now. Perhaps it's a sort of instinct; but I rather think it is the result of an unconscious absorption of a number of little indications about me. Be it as it may, I am resolved to leave no opening to the enemy if I can help it, and I want you to see if you can suggest any further precautions beyond those I am taking. Come and look at the stables."

Dorrington could see no opening for any piece of rascality by which he might make more of the case than by serving his client loyally, so he resolved to do the latter. He followed Mr. Telfer through the training stables, where eight or nine thoroughbreds stood, and could suggest no improvement upon the exceptional precautions that already existed.

"No," said Dorrington, "I don't think you can do any better than this—at least on this, the inner line of defence. But it is best to make the outer lines secure first. By the way, *this* isn't Janissary, is it? We saw him farther up the row, didn't we?"

"Oh no, that's a very different sort of colt, though he does look like, doesn't he? People who've been up and down the stables once or twice often confuse them. They're both bays, much of a build, and about the same height, and both have a bit of stocking on the same leg, though Janissary's is bigger, and this animal has a white star. But you never saw two creatures look so like and run so differently. This is a dead loss—not worth his feed. If I can manage to wind him up to something like a gallop I shall try to work him off in a selling plate somewhere; but as far as I can see he isn't good enough even for that. He's a disappointment. And his stock's far better than Janissary's too, and he cost half as much again! Yearlings are a lottery. Still, I've drawn a prize or two among them, at one time or another."

"Ah yes, so I've heard. But now as to the outer defences I was speaking of. Let us find out *who* is trying to interfere with your horse. Do you mind letting me into the secrets of the stable commissions?"

"Oh no. We're talking in confidence, of course. I've backed the colt pretty heavily all round, but not too much anywhere. There's a good slice with Barker—you know Barker, of course; Mullins has a thousand down for him, and that was at five to one, before Herald went amiss. Then there's Ford and Lascelles—both good men, and Naylor—he's the smallest man of them all, and there's only a hundred or two with him, though he's been laying the horse pretty freely everywhere, at least until Herald went wrong. And there's Pedder. But there must have been a deal of money laid to outside backers, and there's no telling who may contemplate a ramp."

"Just so. Now as to your nephew. What of your suspicions in that direction?"

"Perhaps I'm a little hasty as to that," Mr. Telfer answered, a little ashamed of what he had previously said. "But I'm worried and mystified, as you see, and hardly know what to think. My nephew Richard is a little erratic, and he has a foolish habit of betting more than he can afford. He and I quarrelled some time back, while he was staying here, because I had an idea that he had been talking too freely outside. He had, in fact; and I regarded it as a breach of confidence. So there was a quarrel and he went away."

"Very well. I wonder if I can get a bed at the 'Crown,' at Redbury? I'm afraid it'll be crowded, but I'll try."

"But why trouble? Why not stay with me, and be near the stables?"

"Because then I should be of no more use to you than one of your lads. People who come out here every morning are probably staying at Redbury, and I must go there after them."

III

The "Crown" at Redbury was full in anticipation of the races, but Dorrington managed to get a room ordinarily occupied by one of the landlord's family, who undertook to sleep at a friend's for a night or two. This settled, he strolled into the yard, and soon fell into animated talk with the hostler on the subject of the forthcoming races. All the town was backing Janissary for the Stakes, the hostler said, and he advised Dorrington to do the same.

During this conversation two men stopped in the street, just outside the yard gate, talking. One was a big, heavy, vulgar-looking fellow in a box-cloth coat, and with a shaven face and hoarse voice; the other was a slighter, slimmer, younger and more gentlemanlike man, though there was a certain patchy colour about his face that seemed to hint of anything but teetotalism.

"There," said the hostler, indicating the younger of these two men, "that's young Mr. Telfer, him as whose uncle's owner o' Janissary. He's a young plunger, he is, and he's on Janissary too. He give me the tip, straight, this mornin'. 'You put your little bit on my uncle's colt,' he said. 'It's all right. I ain't such pals with the old man as I was, but I've got the tip that *his* money's down on it. So don't neglect your opportunities, Thomas,' he says; and I haven't. He's stoppin' in our house, is young Mr. Richard."

"And who is that he is talking to? A bookmaker?"

"Yes, sir, that's Naylor—Bob Naylor. He's got Mr. Richard's bets. P'raps he's puttin' on a bit more now."

The men at the gate separated, and the bookmaker walked off down the street in the fast gathering dusk. Richard Telfer, however, entered the house, and Dorrington followed him. Telfer mounted the stairs and went into his room. Dorrington lingered a moment on the stairs and then went and knocked at Telfer's door.

"Hullo!" cried Telfer, coming to the door and peering out into the gloomy corridor.

"I beg pardon," Dorrington replied courteously. "I thought this was Naylor's room."

"No—it's No. 23, by the end. But I believe he's just gone down the street."

Dorrington expressed his thanks and went to his own room. He took one or two small instruments from his bag and hurried stealthily to the door of No. 23.

All was quiet, and the door opened at once to Dorrington's picklock, for there was nothing but the common tumbler rim-lock to secure it. Dorrington, being altogether an unscrupulous scoundrel, would have thought nothing of entering a man's room thus for purposes of mere robbery. Much less scruple had he in doing so in the present circumstances. He lit the candle in a little pocket lantern, and, having secured the door, looked quickly about the room. There was nothing unusual to attract his attention, and he turned to two bags lying near the dressing-table. One was the usual bookmaker's satchel, and the other was a leather travelling-bag; both were locked. Dorrington unbuckled the straps of the large bag, and produced a slender picklock of steel wire, with a sliding joint, which, with a little skilful "humouring," turned the lock in the course of a minute or two. One glance inside was enough. There on the top lay a large false beard of strong red, and upon the shirts below was a pair of spectacles. But Dorrington went farther, and felt carefully below the linen till his hand met a small, flat, mahogany box. This he withdrew and opened. Within, on a velvet lining, lay a small silver instrument resembling a syringe. He shut and replaced the box, and, having rearranged the contents of the bag, shut, locked and strapped it, and blew out his light. He had found what he came to look for. In another minute Mr. Bob Naylor's door was locked behind him, and Dorrington took his picklocks to his own room.

It was a noisy evening in the Commercial Room at the "Crown." Chaff and laughter flew thick, and Richard Telfer threatened Naylor with a terrible settling day. More was drunk than thirst strictly justified, and everybody grew friendly with everybody else. Dorrington, sober and keenly alert, affected the reverse, and exhibited especial and extreme affection for Mr. Bob Naylor. His advances were unsuccessful at first, but Dorrington's manner and the "Crown" whisky overcame the bookmaker's reserve, and at about eleven o'clock the two left the house arm in arm for a cooling stroll in the High Street. Dorrington blabbed and chattered with great success, and soon began about Janissary.

"So you've pretty well done all you want with Janissary, eh? Book full? Ah! nothing like keeping a book even all round—it's the safest way—'specially with such a colt as Janissary about. Eh, my boy?" He nudged Naylor genially. "Ah! no doubt it's a good colt, but old Telfer has rum notions about preparation, hasn't he?"

"I dunno," replied Naylor. "How do you mean?"

"Why, what does he have the horse led up and down behind the stable for, half an hour every afternoon?"

"Didn't know he did."

"Ah! but he does. I came across it only this afternoon. I was coming over the downs, and just as I got round behind Telfer's stables there I saw a fine bay colt, with a white stocking on the off hind leg, well covered up in a suit of clothes, being led up and down by a lad, like a sentry—up and down, up and down—about twenty yards each way, and nobody else about. 'Hullo!' says I to the lad, 'hullo! what horse is this?' 'Janissary,' says the boy—pretty free for a stable-lad. 'Ah!' says I. 'And what are you walking him like that for?' 'Dunno,' says the boy, 'but it's guv'nor's orders. Every afternoon, at two to the minute, I have to bring him out here and walk him like this for half an hour exactly, neither more nor less, and then he goes in and has a handful of malt. But I dunno why.' 'Well,' says I, 'I never heard of that being done before. But he's a fine colt,' and I put my hand under the cloth and felt him—hard as nails and smooth as silk."

"And the boy let you touch him?"

"Yes; he struck me as a bit easy for a stable-boy. But it's an odd trick, isn't it, that of the half-hour's walk and the handful of malt? Never hear of anybody else doing it, did you?"

"No, I never did."

They talked and strolled for another quarter of an hour, and then finished up with one more drink.

IV

THE NEXT WAS THE DAY before the race, and in the morning Dorrington, making a circuit, came to Mr. Warren Telfer's from the farther side. As soon as they were assured of privacy: "Have you seen the man with the red beard this morning?" asked Dorrington.

"No; I looked out pretty sharply, too."

"That's right. If you like to fall in with my suggestions, however, you shall see him at about two o'clock, and take a handsome rise out of him."

"Very well," Mr. Telfer replied. "What's your suggestion?"

"I'll tell you. In the first place, what's the value of that other horse that looks so like Janissary?"

"Hamid is his name. He's worth—well, what he will fetch. I'll sell him for fifty and be glad of the chance."

"Very good. Then you'll no doubt be glad to risk his health temporarily to make sure of the Redbury Stakes, and to get longer prices for anything you may like to put on between now and to-morrow afternoon. Come to the stables and I'll tell you. But first, is there a place where we may command a view of the ground behind the stables without being seen?"

"Yes, there's a ventilation grating at the back of each stall."

"Good! Then we'll watch from Hamid's stall, which will be empty. Select your most wooden-faced and most careful boy, and send him out behind the stable with Hamid at two o'clock to the moment. Put the horse in a full suit of clothes—it is necessary to cover up that white star—and tell the lad he must *lead* it up and down slowly for twenty yards or so. I rather expect the red-bearded man will be coming along between two o'clock and half-past two. You will understand that Hamid is to be Janissary for the occasion. You must drill your boy to appear a bit of a fool, and to overcome his stable education sufficiently to chatter freely—so long as it is the proper chatter. The man may ask the horse's name, or he may not. Any way, the boy mustn't forget it is Janissary he is leading. You have an odd fad, you must know (and the boy must know it too) in the matter of training. This ridiculous fad is to have your colt walked up and down for half an hour exactly at two o'clock every afternoon, and then given a handful of malt as he comes in. The boy can talk as freely about this as he pleases, and also about the colt's chances, and anything else he likes; and he is to let the stranger come up, talk to the horse, pat him—in short, to do as he pleases. Is that plain?"

"Perfectly. You have found out something about this red-bearded chap then?"

"Oh, yes—it's Naylor the bookmaker, as a matter of fact, with a false beard."

"What! Naylor?"

"Yes. You see the idea, of course. Once Naylor thinks he has nobbled the favourite he will lay it to any extent, and the odds will get longer. Then you can make him pay for his little games."

"Well, yes, of course. Though I wouldn't put too much with Naylor in any case. He's not a big man, and he might break and lose me the lot. But I can get it out of the others."

"Just so. You'd better see about schooling your boy now, I think. I'll tell you more presently."

A minute or two before two o'clock Dorrington and Telfer, mounted on a pair of steps, were gazing through the ventilation grating of Hamid's stall, while the colt, clothed completely, was led round. Then Dorrington described his operations of the previous evening.

"No matter what he may think of my tale," he said, "Naylor will be pretty sure to come. He has tried to bribe your stablemen, and has been baffled. Every attempt to get hold of the boy in charge of Janissary has failed, and he will be glad to clutch at any shadow of a chance to save his money now. Once he is here, and the favourite apparently at his mercy, the thing is done. By the way, I expect your nephew's little present to the man you sacked was a fairly innocent one. No doubt he merely asked the man whether Janissary was keeping well, and was thought good enough to win, for I find he is backing it pretty heavily. Naylor came afterwards, with much less innocent intentions, but fortunately you were down on him in time. Several considerations induced me to go to Naylor's room. In the first place, I have heard rather shady tales of his doings on one or two occasions, and he did not seem a sufficiently big man to stand to lose a great deal over your horse. Then, when I saw him, I observed that his figure bore a considerable resemblance to that of the man you had described, except as regards the red beard and the spectacles—articles easily enough assumed, and, indeed, often enough used by the scum of the ring whose trade is welshing. And, apart from these considerations, here, at any rate, was one man who had an interest in keeping your colt from winning, and here was his room waiting for me to explore. So I explored it, and the card turned up trumps."

As he was speaking, the stable-boy, a stolid-looking youngster, was leading Hamid back and forth on the turf before their eyes.

"There's somebody," said Dorrington suddenly, "over in that clump of trees. Yes—our man, sure enough. I felt pretty sure of him after you had told me that he hadn't thought it worth while to turn up this morning. Here he comes."

Naylor, with his red beard sticking out over the collar of his big coat, came slouching along with an awkwardly assumed air of carelessness and absence of mind.

"Hullo!" he said suddenly, as he came abreast of the horse, turning as though but now aware of its presence, "that's a valuable sort of horse, ain't it, my lad?"

"Yes," said the boy, "it is. He's goin' to win the Redbury Stakes tomorrow. It's Janissary."

"Oh! Janey Sairey, is it?" Naylor answered, with a quaint affectation of gaping ignorance. "Janey Sairey, eh? Well, she do look a fine 'orse, what I can see of 'er. What a suit o' clo'es! An' so she's one o' the 'orses that runs in races, is she? Well, I never! Pretty much like other 'orses, too, to look at, ain't she? Only a bit thin in the legs."

The boy stood carelessly by the colt's side, and the man approached. His hand came quickly from an inner pocket, and then he passed it under Hamid's cloths, near the shoulder. "Ah, it do feel a lovely skin, to be sure!" he said. "An' so there's goin' to be races at Redbury to-morrow, is there? I dunno anythin' about races myself, an'—Oo my!"

Naylor sprang back as the horse, flinging back its ears, started suddenly, swung round, and reared. "Lor," he said, "what a vicious brute! Jist because I stroked her! I'll be careful about touching racehorses again." His hand passed stealthily to the pocket again, and he hurried on his way, while the stable-boy steadied and soothed Hamid.

Telfer and Dorrington sniggered quietly in their concealment. "He's taken a deal of trouble, hasn't he?" Dorrington remarked. "It's a sad case of the biter bit for Mr. Naylor, I'm afraid. That was a prick the colt felt—hypodermic injection with the syringe I saw in the bag, no doubt. The boy won't be such a fool as to come in again at once, will he? If Naylor's taking a look back from anywhere, that may make him suspicious."

"No fear. I've told him to keep out for the half-hour, and he'll do it. Dear, dear, what an innocent person Mr. Bob Naylor is! 'Well, I never! Pretty much like other horses!' He didn't know there were to be races at Redbury! 'Janey Sairey,' too—it's really very funny!"

Ere the half-hour was quite over, Hamid came stumbling and dragging into the stable yard, plainly all amiss, and collapsed on his litter as soon as he gained his stall. There he lay, shivering and drowsy.

"I expect he'll get over it in a day or two," Dorrington remarked. "I don't suppose a vet. could do much for him just now, except, perhaps, give him a drench and let him take a rest. Certainly, the effect will last over to-morrow. That's what it is calculated for."

V

THE REDBURY STAKES WERE RUN at three in the afternoon, after two or three minor events had been disposed of. The betting had undergone considerable fluctuations during the morning, but in general it ruled heavily against Janissary. The story had got about, too, that Mr. Warren Telfer's colt would not start. So that when the numbers went up, and it was seen that Janissary was starting after all, there was much astonishment, and a good deal of uneasiness in the ring.

"It's a pity we can't see our friend Naylor's face just now, isn't it?" Dorrington remarked to his client, as they looked on from Mr. Telfer's drag.

"Yes; it would be interesting," Telfer replied. "He was quite confident last night, you say."

"Quite. I tested him by an offer of a small bet on your colt, asking some points over the odds, and he took it at once. Indeed, I believe he has been going about gathering up all the wagers he could about Janissary, and the market has felt it. Your nephew has risked some more with him, I believe, and altogether it looks as though the town would spoil the 'bookies' badly."

As the horses came from the weighing enclosure, Janissary was seen conspicuous among them, bright, clean, and firm, and a good many faces lengthened at the sight. The start was not so good as it might have been, but the favourite (the starting-price had gone to evens) was not left, and got away well in the crowd of ten starters. There he lay till rounding the bend, when the Telfer blue and chocolate was seen among the foremost, and near the rails. Mr. Telfer almost trembled as he watched through his glasses.

"Hang that Willett!" he said, almost to himself. "He's *too* clever against those rails before getting clear. All right, though, all right! He's coming!"

Janissary, indeed, was showing in front, and as the horses came along the straight it was plain that Mr. Telfer's colt was holding the field comfortably. There were changes in the crowd; some dropped away, some came out and attempted to challenge for the lead, but the favourite, striding easily, was never seriously threatened, and in the end, being a little let out, came in a three-lengths winner, never once having been made to show his best.

"I congratulate you, Mr. Telfer," said Dorrington, "and you may congratulate me."

"Certainly, certainly," said Mr. Telfer hastily, hurrying off to lead in the winner.

It was a bad race for the ring, and in the open parts of the course many a humble fielder grabbed his satchel ere the shouting was over, and made his best pace for the horizon; and more than one pair of false whiskers, as red as Naylor's, came off suddenly while the owner betook himself to a fresh stand. Unless a good many outsiders sailed home before the end of the week there would be a bad Monday for layers. But all sporting Redbury was jubilant. They had all been "on" the local favourite for the local race, and it had won.

VI

Mr. Bob Naylor "got a bit back," in his own phrase, on other races by the end of the week, but all the same he saw a black settling day ahead. He had been done—done for a certainty. He had realised this as soon as he saw the numbers go up for the Redbury Stakes. Janissary had not been drugged after all. That meant that another horse had been substituted for him, and that the whole thing was an elaborate plant. He thought he knew Janissary pretty well by sight, too, and rather prided himself on having an eye for a horse. But clearly it was a plant—a complete do. Telfer was in it, and so of course was that gentlemanly stranger who had strolled along Redbury High Street with him that night, telling that cock-and-bull story about the afternoon walks and the handful of malt. There was a nice schoolboy tale to take in a man who thought himself broad as Cheapside! He cursed himself high and low. To be done, and to know it, was a galling thing, but this would be worse. The tale would get about. They would boast of a clever stroke like that, and that would injure him with everybody; with honest men, because his reputation, as it was, would bear no worsening, and with knaves like himself, because they would laugh at him, and leave him out when any little co-operative swindle was in contemplation. But though the chagrin of the defeat was bitter bad enough, his losses were worse. He had taken everything offered on Janissary after he had nobbled the wrong horse, and had given almost any odds demanded.

Do as he might, he could see nothing but a balance against him on Monday, which, though he might pay out his last cent, he could not cover by several hundred pounds.

But on the day he met his customers at his club, as usual, and paid out freely. Young Richard Telfer, however, with whom he was heavily "in," he put off till the evening. "I've been a bit disappointed this morning over some ready that was to be paid over," he said, "and I've used the last cheque-form in my book. You might come and have a bit of dinner with me to-night, Mr. Telfer, and take it then."

Telfer assented without difficulty.

"All right, then, that's settled. You know the place—Gold Street. Seven sharp. The missis 'll be pleased to see you, I'm sure, Mr. Telfer. Let's see—it's fifteen hundred and thirty altogether, isn't it?"

"Yes, that's it. I'll come."

Young Telfer left the club, and at the corner of the street ran against Dorrington. Telfer, of course, knew him but as his late fellow-guest at the "Crown" at Redbury, and this was their first meeting in London after their return from the races.

"Ah!" said Telfer. "Going to draw a bit of Janissary money, eh?"

"Oh, I haven't much to draw," Dorrington answered. "But I expect your pockets are pretty heavy, if you've just come from Naylor."

"Yes, I've just come from Naylor, but I haven't touched the merry sovs. just yet," replied Telfer cheerfully. "There's been a run on Naylor, and I'm going to dine with him and his respectable missis this evening, and draw the plunder then. I feel rather curious to see what sort of establishment a man like Naylor keeps going. His place is in Gold Street, Chelsea."

"Yes, I believe so. Anyhow, I congratulate you on your haul, and wish you a merry evening." And the two men parted.

Dorrington had, indeed, a few pounds to draw as the result of his "fishing" bet with Naylor, but now he resolved to ask for the money at his own time. This invitation to Telfer took his attention, and it reminded him oddly of the circumstances detailed in the report of the inquest on Lawrence, transcribed at the beginning of this paper. He had cut out this report at the time it appeared, because he saw certain singularities about the case, and he had filed it, as he had done hundreds of other such cuttings. And now certain things led him to fancy that he might be much interested to observe the proceedings at Naylor's house on the evening after a bad settling-day. He resolved to gratify himself with a strict professional watch in Gold Street that evening, on chance of something coming of it. For it was an important thing in Dorrington's rascally trade to get hold of as much of other people's private business as possible, and to know exactly in what cupboard to find every man's skeleton. For there was no knowing but it might be turned into money sooner or later. So he found the number of Naylor's house from the handiest directory, and at six o'clock, a little disguised by a humbler style of dress than usual, he began his watch.

Naylor's house was at the corner of a turning, with the flank wall blank of windows, except for one at the top; and a public-house stood at the opposite corner. Dorrington, skilled in watching without attracting attention to himself, now lounged in the public-house bar, now stood at the street corner, and now sauntered along the street, a picture of vacancy of mind, and looking, apparently, at everything in turn, except the house at the corner. The first thing he noted was the issuing forth from the area steps of a healthy-looking girl in much gaily be-ribboned finery. Plainly a servant taking an evening out. This was an odd thing, that a servant should be allowed out on an evening when a guest was expected to dinner; and the house looked like one where it was more likely that one servant would be kept than two. Dorrington hurried after the girl, and, changing his manner of address to that of a civil labourer, said—

"Beg pardon, Miss, but is Mary Walker still in service at your 'ouse?"

"Mary Walker?" said the girl. "Why, no. I never 'eard the name. And there ain't nobody in service there but me."

"Beg pardon—it must be the wrong 'ouse. It's my cousin, Miss, that's all."

Dorrington left the girl and returned to the public-house. As he reached it he perceived a second noticeable thing. Although it was broad daylight, there was now a light behind the solitary window at the top of the side-wall of Naylor's house. Dorrington slipped through the swing-doors of the public-house and watched through the glass.

It was a bare room behind the high window—it might have been a bathroom—and its interior was made but dimly visible from outside by the light. A tall, thin woman was setting up an ordinary pair of house-steps in the middle of the room. This done, she turned to the window and pulled down the blind, and as she did so Dorrington noted her very extreme thinness, both of face and body. When the blind was down the light still remained within. Again there seemed some significance in this. It appeared that the thin woman had waited until her servant had gone before doing whatever she had to do in that room. Presently the watcher came again into Gold Street, and from there caught a passing glimpse of the thin woman as she moved busily about the front room over the breakfast parlour.

Clearly, then, the light above had been left for future use. Dorrington thought for a minute, and then suddenly stopped, with a snap of the fingers. He saw it all now. Here was something altogether in his way. He would take a daring course.

He withdrew once more to the public-house, and ordering another drink, took up a position in a compartment from which he could command a view both of Gold Street and the side turning. The time now, he saw by his watch, was ten minutes to seven. He had to wait rather more than a quarter of an hour before seeing Richard Telfer come walking jauntily down Gold Street, mount the steps, and knock at Naylor's door. There was a momentary glimpse of the thin woman's face at the door, and then Telfer entered.

It now began to grow dusk, and in about twenty minutes more Dorrington took to the street again. The room over the breakfast-parlour was clearly the dining-room. It was lighted brightly, and by intent listening the watcher could distinguish, now and again, a sudden burst of laughter from Telfer, followed by the deeper grunts of Naylor's voice, and once by sharp tones that it seemed natural to suppose were the thin woman's.

Dorrington waited no longer, but slipped a pair of thick sock-feet over his shoes, and, after a quick look along the two streets, to make sure nobody was near, he descended the area steps. There was no light in the breakfast-parlour. With his knife he opened the window-catch, raised the sash quietly and stepped over the sill, and stood in the dark room within.

All was quiet, except for the talking in the room above. He had done but what many thieves—"parlour-jumpers"—do every day; but there was more ahead. He made his way silently to the basement passage, and passed into the kitchen. The room was lighted, and cookery utensils were scattered about, but nobody was there. He waited till he heard a request in Naylor's gruff voice for "another slice" of something, and noiselessly mounted the stairs. He noticed that the dining-room door was ajar, but passed quickly on to the second flight, and rested on the landing above. Mrs. Naylor would probably have to go downstairs once or twice again, but he did not expect anybody in the upper part of the house just yet. There was a small flight of stairs above the landing whereon he stood, leading to the servant's bedroom and the bathroom. He took a glance at the bathroom with its feeble lamp, its steps, and its open ceiling-trap, and returned again to the bedroom landing. There he stood, waiting watchfully.

Twice the thin woman emerged from the dining-room, went downstairs and came up again, each time with food and plates. Then she went down once more, and was longer gone. Meantime Naylor and Telfer were talking and joking loudly at the table.

When once again Dorrington saw the crown of the thin woman's head rising over the bottom stair, he perceived that she bore a tray set with cups already filled with coffee. These she carried into the dining-room, whence presently came the sound of striking matches. After this the conversation seemed to flag, and Telfer's part in it grew less and less, till it ceased altogether, and the house was silent, except for a sound of heavy breathing. Soon this became almost a snore, and then there was a sudden noisy tumble, as of a drunken man; but still the snoring went on, and the Naylors were talking in whispers.

There was a shuffling and heaving sound, and a chair was knocked over. Then at the dining-room door appeared Naylor, walking backward, and carrying the inert form of Telfer by the shoulders, while the thin woman followed, supporting the feet. Dorrington retreated up the small stair-flight, cocking a pocket revolver as he went.

Up the stairs they came, Naylor puffing and grunting with the exertion, and Telfer still snoring soundly on, till at last, having mounted the top flight, they came in at the bathroom door, where Dorrington stood to receive them, smiling and bowing pleasantly, with his hat in one hand and his revolver in the other.

The woman, from her position, saw him first, and dropped Telfer's legs with a scream. Naylor turned his head and then also dropped his end. The drugged man fell in a heap, snoring still.

Naylor, astounded and choking, made as if to rush at the interloper, but Dorrington thrust the revolver into his face, and exclaimed, still smiling courteously, "Mind, mind! It's a dangerous thing, is a revolver, and apt to go off if you run against it!"

He stood thus for a second, and then stepped forward and took the woman—who seemed like to swoon—by the arm, and pulled her into the room. "Come, Mrs. Naylor," he said, "you're not one of the fainting sort, and I think I'd better keep two such clever people as you under my eye, or one of you may get into mischief. Come now, Naylor, we'll talk business."

Naylor, now white as a ghost, sat on the edge of the bath, and stared at Dorrington as though in a fascination of terror. His hands rested on the bath at each side, and an odd sound of gurgling came from his thick throat.

"We will talk business," Dorrington resumed. "Come, you've met me before now, you know—at Redbury. You can't have forgotten Janissary, and the walking exercise and the handful of malt. I'm afraid you're a clumsy sort of rascal, Naylor, though you do your best. I'm a rascal myself (though I don't often confess it), and I assure you that your conceptions are crude as yet. Still, that isn't a bad notion in its way, that of drugging a man and drowning him in your cistern up there in the roof, when you prefer not to pay him his winnings. It has the very considerable merit that, after the body has been fished out of any river you may choose to fling it into, the stupid coroner's jury will never suspect that it was drowned in any other water but that. Just as happened in the Lawrence case, for instance. You remember that, eh? So do I, very well, and it was because I remembered that that I paid you this visit to-night. But you do the thing much too clumsily, really. When I saw a light up here in broad daylight I knew at once it must be left for some purpose to be executed later in the evening; and when I saw the steps carefully placed at the same time, after the servant had been sent out, why the thing was plain, remembering, as I did, the curious coincidence that Mr. Lawrence was drowned the very evening he had been here to take away his winnings. The steps *must* be intended to give access to the roof, where there was probably a tank to feed the bath, and what more secret place to drown a man than there? And what easier place, so long as the man was well drugged, and there was a strong lid to the tank? As I say, Naylor, your notion was meritorious, but your execution was wretched—perhaps because you had no notion that I was watching you."

He paused, and then went on. "Come," he said, "collect your scattered faculties, both of you. I shan't hand you over to the police for this little invention of yours; it's too useful an invention to give away to the police. I shan't hand you over, that is to say, as long as you do as I tell you. If you get mutinous, you shall hang, both of you, for the Lawrence business. I may as well tell you that I'm a bit of a scoundrel myself, by way of profession. I don't boast about it, but it's well to be frank in making arrangements of this sort. I'm going to take you into my service. I employ a few agents, and you and your tank may come in very handy from time to time. But we must set it up, with a few improvements, in another house—a house which hasn't quite such an awkward window. And we mustn't execute our little suppressions so regularly on settling-day; it looks suspicious. So as soon as you can get your faculties together we'll talk over this thing."

The man and the woman had exchanged glances during this speech, and now Naylor asked, huskily, jerking his thumb toward the man on the floor, "An'—an' what about 'im?"

"What about him? Why, get rid of him as soon as you like. Not that way, though." (He pointed toward the ceiling trap.) "It doesn't pay *me*, and I'm master now. Besides, what will people say when you tell the same tale at his inquest that you told at Lawrence's? No, my friend, bookmaking and murder don't assort together, profitable as the combination may seem. Settling-days are too regular. And I'm not going to be your accomplice, mind. You are going to be mine. Do what you please with Telfer. Leave him on somebody's doorstep if you like."

"But I owe him fifteen hundred, and I ain't got more than half of it! I'll be ruined!"

"Very likely," Dorrington returned placidly. "Be ruined as soon as possible, then, and devote all your time to my business. You're not to ornament the ring any longer, remember—you're to assist a private inquiry agent, you and your wife and your charming tank. Repudiate the debt if you like—it's a mere gaming transaction, and there is no legal claim—or leave him in the street and tell him he's been robbed. Please yourself as to this little roguery—you may as well, for it's the last you will do on your own account. For the future your respectable talents will be devoted to the service of Dorrington & Hicks, private inquiry agents; and if you don't give satisfaction, that eminent firm will hang you, with the assistance of the judge at the Old Bailey. So settle your business yourselves, and quickly, for I've a good many things to arrange with you."

And, Dorrington watching them continually, they took Telfer out by the side gate in the garden wall and left him in a dark corner.

THUS I LEARNT THE HISTORY of the horrible tank that had so nearly ended my own life, as I have already related. Clearly the Naylors had changed their name to Crofting on taking compulsory service with Dorrington, and Mrs. Naylor was the repulsively thin woman who had drugged me with her coffee in the house at Highgate. The events I have just recorded took place about three years before I came to England. In the meantime how many people, whose deaths might be turned to profit, had fallen victims to the murderous cunning of Dorrington and his tools?

III

THE CASE OF THE "MIRROR OF PORTUGAL"

I

WHETHER OR NOT THIS CASE has an historical interest is a matter of conjecture. If it has none, then the title I have given it is a misnomer. But I think the conjecture that some historical interest attaches to it is by no means an empty one, and all that can be urged against it is the common though not always declared error that romance expired fifty years at least ago, and history with it. This makes it seem improbable that the answer to an unsolved riddle of a century since should be found to-day in an inquiry agent's dingy office in Bedford Street, Covent Garden. Whether or not it has so been found the reader may judge for himself, though the evidence stops far short of actual proof of the identity of the "Mirror of Portugal" with the stone wherewith this case was concerned.

But first, as to the "Mirror of Portugal." This was a diamond of much and ancient fame. It was of Indian origin, and it had lain in the possession of the royal family of Portugal in the time of Portugal's ancient splendour. But three hundred years ago, after the extinction of the early line of succession, the diamond, with other jewels, fell into the possession of Don Antonio, one of the half-dozen pretenders who were then scrambling for the throne. Don Antonio, badly in want of money, deposited the stone in pledge with Queen Elizabeth of England, and never redeemed it. Thus it took its place as one of the English Crown jewels, and so remained till the overthrow and death of Charles the First. Queen Henrietta then carried it with her to France, and there, to obtain money to satisfy her creditors, she sold it to the great Cardinal Mazarin. He bequeathed it, at his death, to the French Crown, and among the Crown jewels of France it once more found a temporary abiding place. But once more it brought disaster with it in the shape of a revolution, and again a king lost his head at the executioner's hands. And in the riot and confusion of the great Revolution of 1792 the "Mirror of Portugal," with other jewels, vanished utterly. Where it went to, and who took it, nobody ever knew. The "Mirror of Portugal" disappeared as suddenly and effectually as though fused to vapour by electric combustion.

So much for the famous "Mirror." Whether or not its history is germane to the narrative which follows, probably nobody will ever certainly know. But that Dorrington considered that it was, his notes on the case abundantly testify.

For some days before Dorrington's attention was in any way given to this matter, a poorly-dressed and not altogether prepossessing Frenchman had been haunting the staircase and tapping at the office door, unsuccessfully attempting an interview with Dorrington, who happened to be out, or busy, whenever he called. The man never asked for Hicks, Dorrington's partner; but this was very natural. In the first place, it was always Dorrington who met all strangers and conducted all negotiations, and in the second, Dorrington had just lately, in a case regarding a secret society in Soho, made his name much known and respected, not to say feared, in the foreign colony of that quarter; wherefore it was likely that a man who bore evidence of residence in that neighbourhood should come with the name of Dorrington on his tongue.

The weather was cold, but the man's clothes were thin and threadbare, and he had no overcoat. His face was of a broad, low type, coarse in feature and small in forehead, and he wore the baggy black linen peaked cap familiar on the heads of men of his class in parts of Paris. He had called unsuccessfully, as I have said, sometimes once, sometimes more frequently, on each of three or four days before he succeeded in seeing Dorrington. At last, however, he intercepted him on the stairs, as Dorrington arrived at about eleven in the morning.

"Pardon, m'sieu," he said, laying his finger on Dorrington's arm, "it is M. Dorrington—not?"

"Well—suppose it is, what then?" Dorrington never admitted his identity to a stranger without first seeing good cause.

"I 'ave beesness—very great beesness; beesness of a large profit for you if you please to take it. Where shall I tell it?"

"Come in here," Dorrington replied, leading the way to his private room. The man did not look like a wealthy client, but that signified nothing. Dorrington had made profitable strokes after introductions even less promising.

The man followed Dorrington, pulled off his cap, and sat in the chair Dorrington pointed at.

"In the first place," said Dorrington, "what's your name?"

"Ah, yas—but before—all that I tell is for ourselves alone, is it not? It is all in confidence, eh?"

"Yes, yes, of course," Dorrington answered, with virtuous impatience. "Whatever is said in this room is regarded as strictly confidential. What's your name?"

"Jacques Bouvier."

"Living at—?"

"Little Norham Street, Soho."

"And now the business you speak of."

"The beesness is this. My cousin, Léon Bouvier—he is *coquin*—a rrrascal!"

"Very likely."

"He has a great jewel—it is, I have no doubt, a diamond—of a great value. It is not his! There is no right of him to it! It should be mine. If you get it for me one-quarter of it in money shall be yours! And it is of a great value."

"Where does your cousin live? What is he?"

"Beck Street, Soho. He has a shop—a café—Café des Bons Camarades. And he give me not a crrrust—if I starve!"

It scarcely seemed likely that the keeper of a little foreign café in a back street of Soho would be possessed of a jewel a quarter of whose value would be prize enough to tempt Dorrington to take a new case up. But Dorrington bore with the man a little longer. "What is this jewel you talk of?" he asked. "And if you don't know enough about it to be quite sure whether it is a diamond or not, what *do* you know?"

"Listen! The stone I have never seen; but that it is a diamond makes probable. What else so much value? And it is much value that gives my cousin so great care and trouble—*cochon!* Listen! I relate to you. My father—he was charcoal-burner at Bonneuil, department of Seine. My uncle—the father of my cousin—also was charcoal-burner. The grandfather—charcoal-burner also; and his father and his grandfather before him—all burners of charcoal, at Bonneuil. Now perceive. The father of my grandfather was of the great Revolution—a young man, great among those who stormed the Bastille, the Tuileries, the Hôtel de Ville, brave, and a leader. Now, when palaces were burnt and heads were falling there was naturally much confusion. Things were lost—things of large value. What more natural? While so many were losing the head from the shoulders, it was not strange that some should lose jewels from the neck. And when these things were lost, who might have a greater right to keep them than the young men of the Revolution, the brave, and the leaders, they who did the work?"

"If you mean that your respectable great-grandfather stole something, you needn't explain it any more," Dorrington said. "I quite understand."

"I do not say stole; when there is a great revolution a thing is anybody's. But it would not be convenient to tell of it at the time, for the new Government might believe everything to be its own. These things I do not know, you will understand—I suggest an explanation, that is all. After the great Revolution, my great-grandfather lives alone and quiet, and burns the charcoal as before. Why? The jewel is too great to sell so soon. So he gives it to his son and dies. He also, my grandfather, still burns the charcoal. Again, why? Because, as I believe, he is too poor, too common a man to go about openly to sell so great a stone. More, he loves the stone, for with that he is always rich; and so he burns his charcoal and lives contented as his father had done, and he is rich, and nobody knows it. What then? He has two sons. When he dies, which son does he leave the stone to? Each one says it is for himself—that is natural. I say it was for my father. But however that may make itself, my father dies suddenly. He falls in a pit—by accident, says his brother; not by accident, says my mother; and soon after, she dies too. By accident too, perhaps you ask? Oh yes, by accident too, no doubt." The man laughed disagreeably. "So I am left alone, a little boy, to burn charcoal. When I am a bigger boy there comes the great war, and the Prussians besiege Paris. My uncle, he, burning charcoal no more, goes at night, and takes things from the dead Prussians. Perhaps they are not always quite dead when he finds them—perhaps he makes them so. Be that as it will, the Prussians take him one dark night; and they stand him against a garden wall, and pif! paf! they shoot him. That is all of my uncle; but he dies a rich man, and nobody knows. What does his wife do? She has the jewel, and she has a little money that has been got from the dead Prussians. So when the war is over, she comes to London with my cousin, the bad Léon, and she has the café—Café des Bons Camarades. And Léon grows up, and his mother dies, and he has the café, and with the jewel is a rich man—nobody knowing; nobody but me. But, figure to yourself; shall I burn charcoal and starve at Bonneuil with a rich cousin in London—rich with a diamond that should be mine? Not so. I come over, and Léon, at first he lets me wait at the café. But I do not want that—there is the stone, and I can never see it, never find it. So one day Léon finds me looking in a box, and—chut! out I go. I tell Léon that I will share the jewel with him or I will tell the police. He laughs at me—there is no jewel, he says—I am mad. I do not tell the police, for that is to lose it altogether. But I come here and I offer you one quarter of the diamond if you shall get it."

"Steal it for you, eh?"

Jacques Bouvier shrugged his shoulders. "The word is as you please," he said. "The jewel is not his. And if there is delay it will be gone. Already he goes each day to Hatton Garden, leaving his wife to keep the Café des Bons Camarades. Perhaps he is selling the jewel to-day! Who can tell? So that it will be well that you begin at once."

"Very well. My fee in advance will be twenty guineas."

"What? *Dieu!*—I have no money, I tell you! Get the diamond, and there is one quarter—twenty-five per cent.—for you!"

"But what guarantee do you give that this story of yours isn't all a hoax? Can you expect me to take everything on trust, and work for nothing?"

The man rose and waved his arms excitedly. "It is true, I say!" he exclaimed. "It is a fortune! There is much for you, and it will pay! I have no money, or you should have some. What can I do? You will lose the chance if you are foolish!"

"It rather seems to me, my friend, that I shall be foolish to give valuable time to gratifying your cock-and-bull fancies. See here now. I'm a man of business, and my time is fully occupied. You come here and waste half an hour or more of it with a long rigmarole about some valuable article that you say yourself you have never seen, and you don't even know whether it is a diamond or not. You wander at large over family traditions which you may believe yourself or may not. You have no money, and you offer no fee as a guarantee of your *bonâ fides*, and the sum of the thing is that you ask me to go and commit a theft—to purloin an article you can't even describe, and then to give you three-quarters of the proceeds. No, my man, you have made a mistake. You must go away from here at once, and if I find you hanging about my door again I shall have you taken away very summarily. Do you understand? Now go away."

"*Mon Dieu!* But—"

"I've no more time to waste," Dorrington answered, opening the door and pointing to the stairs. "If you stay here any longer you'll get into trouble."

Jacques Bouvier walked out, muttering and agitating his hands. At the top stair he turned and, almost too angry for words, burst out, "Sir—you are a ver' big fool—a fool!" But Dorrington slammed the door.

He determined, however, if he could find a little time, to learn a little more of Léon Bouvier—perhaps to put a man to watch at the Café des Bons Camarades. That the keeper of this place in Soho should go regularly to Hatton Garden, the diamond market, was curious, and Dorrington had met and analysed too many extraordinary romances to put aside unexamined Jacques Bouvier's seemingly improbable story. But, having heard all the man had to say, it had clearly been his policy to get rid of him in the way he had done. Dorrington was quite ready to steal a diamond, or anything else of value, if it could be done quite safely, but he was no such fool as to give three-quarters of his plunder—or any of it—to somebody else. So that the politic plan was to send Jacques Bouvier away with the impression that his story was altogether pooh-poohed and was to be forgotten.

II

DORRINGTON LEFT HIS OFFICE LATE that day, and the evening being clear, though dark, he walked toward Conduit Street by way of Soho; he thought to take a glance at the Café des Bons Camarades on his way, without being observed, should Jacques Bouvier be in the vicinity.

Beck Street, Soho, was a short and narrow street lying east and west, and joining two of the larger streets that stretch north and south across the district. It was even a trifle dirtier than these by-streets in that quarter are wont to be. The Café des Bons Camarades was a little green-painted shop the window whereof was backed by muslin curtains, while upon the window itself appeared in florid painted letters the words "Cuisine Française." It was the only shop in the street, with the exception of a small coal and firewood shed at one end, the other buildings consisting of the side wall of a factory, now closed for the night, and a few tenement houses. An alley entrance—apparently the gate of a stable-yard—stood next the café. As Dorrington walked by the steamy window, he was startled to hear his own name and some part of his office address spoken in excited tones somewhere in this dark alley entrance; and suddenly a man rather well dressed, and cramming a damaged tall hat on his head as he went, darted from the entrance and ran in the direction from which Dorrington had come. A stoutly built Frenchwoman, carrying on her face every indication of extreme excitement, watched him from the gateway, and Dorrington made no doubt that it was in her voice that he had heard his name mentioned.

He walked briskly to the end of the short street, turned at the end, and hurried round the block of houses, in hope to catch another sight of the man. Presently he saw him, running, in Old Compton Street, and making in the direction of Charing Cross Road. Dorrington mended his pace, and followed. The man emerged where Shaftesbury Avenue meets Charing Cross Road, and, as he crossed, hesitated once or twice, as though he thought of hailing a cab, but decided rather to trust his own legs. He hastened through the byways to St. Martin's Lane, and Dorrington now perceived that one side and half the back of his coat was dripping with wet mud. Also it was plain, as Dorrington had suspected, that his destination was Dorrington's own office in Bedford Street. So the follower broke into a trot, and at last came upon the muddy man wrenching at the bell and pounding at the closed door of the house in Bedford Street, just as the housekeeper began to turn the lock.

"M'sieu Dorrington—M'sieu Dorrington!" the man exclaimed, excitedly, as the door was opened.

"'E's gawn 'ome long ago," the caretaker growled; "you might 'a known that. Oh, 'ere 'e is though—good evenin', sir."

"I am Mr. Dorrington," the inquiry agent said politely. "Can I do anything for you?"

"Ah yes—it is important—at once! I am robbed!"

"Just step upstairs, then, and tell me about it."

Dorrington had but begun to light the gas in his office when his visitor broke out, "I am robbed, M'sieu Dorrington, robbed by my cousin—*coquin!* Rrrobbed of everything! Rrrobbed I tell you!" He seemed astonished to find the other so little excited by the intelligence.

"Let me take your coat," Dorrington said, calmly. "You've had a downer in the mud, I see. Why, what's this?" he smelt the collar as he went toward a hat-peg. "Chloroform!"

"Ah yes—it is that rrrascal Jacques! I will tell you. This evening I go into the gateway next my house—Café des Bons Camarades—to enter by the side-door, and—paf!—a shawl is fling across my face from behind—it is pull tight—there is a knee in my back—I can catch nothing with my hand—it smell all hot in my throat—I choke and I fall over—there is no more. I wake up and I see my wife, and she take me into the house. I am all muddy and tired, but I feel—and I have lost my property—it is a diamond—and my cousin Jacques, he has done it!"

"Are you sure of that?"

"Sure? Oh yes—it is certain, I tell you—certain!"

"Then why not inform the police?"

The visitor was clearly taken aback by this question. He faltered, and looked searchingly in Dorrington's face. "That is not always the convenient way," he said. "I would rather that you do it. It is the diamond that I want—not to punish my cousin—thief that he is!"

Dorrington mended a quill with ostentatious care, saying encouragingly as he did so, "I can quite understand that you may not wish to prosecute your cousin—only to recover the diamond you speak of. Also I can quite understand that there may be reasons—family reasons perhaps, perhaps others—which may render it inadvisable to make even the existence of the jewel known more than absolutely necessary. For instance, there may be other claimants, Monsieur Léon Bouvier."

The visitor started. "You know my name then?" he asked. "How is that?"

Dorrington smiled the smile of a sphinx. "M. Bouvier," he said, "it is my trade to know everything—everything." He put the pen down and gazed whimsically at the other. "My agents are everywhere. You talk of the secret agent of the Russian police—they are nothing. It is my trade to know all things. For instance"—Dorrington unlocked a drawer and produced a book (it was but an office diary), and, turning its pages, went on. "Let me see—B. It is my trade, for instance, to know about the Café des Bons Camarades, established by the late Madame Bouvier, now unhappily deceased. It is my trade to know of Madame Bouvier at Bonneuil, where the charcoal was burnt, and where Madame Bouvier was unfortunately left a widow at the time of the siege of Paris, because of some lamentable misunderstanding of her husband's with a file of Prussian soldiers by an orchard wall. It is my trade, moreover, to know something of the sad death of that husband's brother—in a pit—and of the later death of his widow. Oh yes. More" (turning a page attentively, as though following detailed notes), "it is my trade to know of a little quarrel between those brothers—it might even have been about a diamond, just such a diamond as you have come about to-night—and of jewels missed from the Tuileries in the great Revolution a hundred years ago." He shut the book with a bang and returned it to its place. "And there are other things—too many to talk about," he said, crossing his legs and smiling calmly at the Frenchman.

During this long pretence at reading, Bouvier had slid farther and farther forward on his chair, till he sat on the edge, his eyes staring wide, and his chin dropped. He had been pale when he arrived, but now he was of a leaden gray. He said not a word.

Dorrington laughed lightly. "Come," he said, "I see you are astonished. Very likely. Very few of the people and families whose *dossiers* we have here" (he waved his hand generally about the room) "are aware of what we know. But we don't make a song of it, I assure you, unless it is for the benefit of clients. A client's affairs are sacred, of course, and our resources are at his disposal. Do I understand that you become a client?"

Bouvier sat a little farther back on his chair and closed his mouth. "A—a—yes," he answered at length, with an effort, moistening his lips as he spoke. "That is why I come."

"Ah, now we shall understand each other," Dorrington replied genially, opening an ink-pot and clearing his blotting-pad. "We're not connected with the police here, or anything of that sort, and except so far as we can help them we leave our client's affairs alone. You wish to be a client, and you wish me to recover your lost diamond. Very well, that is business. The first thing is the usual fee in advance—twenty guineas. Will you write a cheque?"

Bouvier had recovered some of his self-possession, and he hesitated. "It is a large fee," he said.

"Large? Nonsense! It is the sort of fee that might easily be swallowed up in half a day's expenses. And besides—a rich diamond merchant like yourself!"

Bouvier looked up quickly. "Diamond merchant?" he said. "I do not understand. I have lost my diamond—there was but one."

"And yet you go to Hatton Garden every day."

"What!" cried Bouvier, letting his hand fall from the table, "you know that too?"

"Of course," Dorrington laughed, easily; "it is my trade, I tell you. But write the cheque."

Bouvier produced a crumpled and dirty cheque-book and complied, with many pauses, looking up dazedly from time to time into Dorrington's face.

"Now," said Dorrington, "tell me where you kept your diamond, and all about it."

"It was in an old little wooden box—so." Bouvier, not yet quite master of himself, sketched an oblong of something less than three inches long by two broad. "The box was old and black—my grandfather may have made it, or his father. The lid fitted very tight, and the inside was packed with fine charcoal powder with the diamond resting in it. The diamond—oh, it was great; like that—so." He made another sketch, roughly square, an inch and a quarter across. "But it looked even much greater still, so bright, so wonderful! It is easy to understand that my grandfather did not sell it—beside the danger. It is so beautiful a thing, and it is such great riches—all in one little box. Why should not a poor charcoal-burner be rich in secret, and look at his diamond, and get all the few things he wants by burning his charcoal? And there was the danger. But that is long ago. I am a man of beesness, and I desired to sell it and be rich. And that Jacques—he has stolen it!"

"Let us keep to the point. The diamond was in a box. Well, where was the box?"

"On the outside of the box there were notches—so, and so. Round the box at each place there was a tight, strong, silk cord—that is two cords. The cords were round my neck, under my shirt, so. And the box was under my arm—just as a boy carries his satchel, but high up—in the armpit, where I could feel it at all times. To-night, when I come to myself, my collar was broken at the stud—see—the cords were cut— and all was gone!"

"You say your cousin Jacques has done this. How do you know?"

"Ah! But who else? Who else could know? And he has always tried to steal it. At first, I let him wait at the Café des Bons Camarades. What does he do? He prys about my house, and opens drawers; and I catch him at last looking in a box, and I turn him out. And he calls me a thief! *Sacré!* He goes—I have no more of him; and so—he does this!"

"Very well. Write down his name and address on this piece of paper, and your own." Bouvier did so. "And now tell me what you have been doing at Hatton Garden."

"Well, it was a very great diamond—I could not go to the first man and show it to sell. I must make myself known."

"It never struck you to get the stone cut in two, did it?"

"Eh? What?—*Nom de chien!* No!" He struck his knee with his hand. "Fool! Why did I not think of that? But still"—he grew more thoughtful—"I should have to show it to get it cut, and I did not know where to go. And the value would have been less."

"Just so—but it's the regular thing to do, I may tell you, in cases like this. But go on. About Hatton Garden, you know."

"I thought that I must make myself known among the merchants of diamonds, and then, perhaps, I should learn the ways, and one day be able to sell. As it was, I knew nothing—nothing at all. I waited, and I saved money in the café. Then, when I could do it, I dressed well and went and bought some diamonds of a dealer—very little diamonds, a little trayful for twenty pounds, and I try to sell them again. But I have paid too much—I can only sell for fifteen pounds. Then I buy more, and sell them for what I give. Then I take an office in Hatton Garden—that is, I share a room with a dealer, and there is a partition between our desks. My wife attends the café, I go to Hatton Garden to buy and sell. It loses me money, but I must lose till I can sell the great diamond. I get to know the dealers more and more, and then to-night, as I go home—" he finished with an expressive shrug and a wave of the hand.

"Yes, yes, I think I see," Dorrington said. "As to the diamond again. It doesn't happen to be a *blue* diamond, does it?"

"No—pure white; perfect."

Dorrington had asked because two especially famous diamonds disappeared from among the French Crown jewels at the time of the great Revolution. One blue, the greatest coloured diamond ever known, and the other the "Mirror of Portugal." Bouvier's reply made it plain that it was certainly not the first which he had just lost.

"Come," Dorrington said, "I will call and inspect the scene of your disaster. I haven't dined yet, and it must be well past nine o'clock now."

They returned to Beck Street. There were gates at the dark entry by the side of the Café des Bons Camarades, but they were never shut, Bouvier explained. Dorrington had them shut now, however, and a lantern was produced. The paving was of rough cobble stones, deep in mud.

"Do many people come down here in the course of an evening?" Dorrington asked.

"Never anybody but myself."

"Very well. Stand away at your side door."

Bouvier and his wife stood huddled and staring on the threshold of the side door, while Dorrington, with the lantern, explored the muddy cobble stones. The pieces of a broken bottle lay in a little heap, and a cork lay a yard away from them. Dorrington smelt the cork, and then collected together the broken glass (there were but four or five pieces) from the little heap. Another piece of glass lay by itself a little way off, and this also Dorrington took up, scrutinising it narrowly. Then he traversed the whole passage carefully, stepping from bare stone to bare stone, and skimming the ground with the lantern. The mud lay confused and trackless in most places, though the place where Bouvier had been lying was indicated by an appearance of sweeping, caused, no doubt, by his wife dragging him to his feet. Only one other thing beside the glass and cork did Dorrington carry away as evidence, and that the Bouviers knew nothing of; for it was the remembrance of the mark of a sharp, small boot-heel in more than one patch of mud between the stones.

"Will you object, Madame Bouvier," he asked, as he handed back the lantern, "to show me the shoes you wore when you found your husband lying out here?"

Madame Bouvier had no objection at all. They were what she was then wearing, and had worn all day. She lifted her foot and exhibited one. There was no need for a second glance. It was a loose easy cashmere boot, with spring sides and heels cut down flat for indoor comfort.

"And this was at what time?"

It was between seven and eight o'clock, both agreed, though they differed a little as to the exact time. Bouvier had recovered when his wife raised him, had entered the house with her, at once discovered his loss, and immediately, on his wife's advice, set out to find Dorrington, whose name the woman had heard spoken of frequently among the visitors to the café in connection with the affair of the secret society already alluded to. He had felt certain that Dorrington would not be at his office, but trusted to be directed where to find him.

"Now," Dorrington asked of Bouvier (the woman had been called away), "tell me some more about your cousin. Where does he live?"

"In Little Norham Street; the third house from this end on the right and the back room at the top. That is unless he has moved just lately."

"Has he been ill recently?"

"Ill?" Bouvier considered. "Not that I can say—no. I have never heard of Jacques being ill." It seemed to strike him as an incongruous and new idea. "Nothing has made him ill all his life—he is too good in constitution, I think."

"Does he wear spectacles?"

"Spectacles? *Mais non!* Never! Why should he wear spectacles? His eyes are good as mine."

"Very well. Now attend. To-morrow you must not go to Hatton

Garden—I will go for you. If you see your cousin Jacques you must say nothing, take no notice; let everything proceed as though nothing had happened; leave all to me. Give me your address at Hatton Garden."

"But what is it you must do there?"

"That is my business. I do my business in my own way. Still I will give you a hint. Where is it that diamonds are sold? In Hatton Garden, as you so well know—as I expect your cousin knows if he has been watching you. Then where will your cousin go to sell it? Hatton Garden, of course. Never mind what I shall do there to intercept it. I am to be your new partner, you understand, bringing money into the business. You must be ill and stay at home till you hear from me. Go now and write me a letter of introduction to the man who shares the office with you. Or I will write it if you like, and you shall sign it. What sort of a man is he?"

"Very quiet—a tall man, perhaps English, but perhaps not."

"Ever buy or sell diamonds with him?"

"Once only. It was the first time. That is how I learned of the half-office to let."

The letter was written, and Dorrington stuffed it carelessly into his pocket. "Mr. Hamer is the name, is it?" he said. "I fancy I have met him somewhere. He is short-sighted, isn't he?"

"Oh yes, he is short-sighted. With *pince-nez*."

"Not very well lately?"

"No—I think not. He takes medicine in the office. But you will be careful, eh? He must not know."

"Do you think so? Perhaps I may tell him, though."

"Tell him? *Ciel*—no! You must not tell people! No!"

"Shall I throw the whole case over, and keep your deposit fee?"

"No—no, not that. But it is foolish to tell to people!"

"I am to judge what is foolish and what wise, M. Bouvier. Good evening!"

"Good evening, M. Dorrington; good evening." Bouvier followed him out to the gate. "And will you tell me—do you think there is a way to get the diamond? Have you any plan?"

"Oh yes, M. Bouvier, I have a plan. But, as I have said, that is my business. It may be a successful plan, or it may not; that we shall see."

"And—and the *dossier*. The notes that you so marvellously have, written out in the book you read. When this business is over you will destroy them, eh? You will not leave a clue?"

"The notes that I have in my books," answered Dorrington, without relaxing a muscle of his face, "are my property, for my own purposes, and were mine before you came to me. Those relating to you are a mere item in thousands. So long as you behave well, M. Bouvier, they will not harm you, and, as I said, the confidences of a client are sacred to Dorrington & Hicks. But as to keeping them—certainly I shall. Once more—good evening!"

Even the stony-faced Dorrington could not repress a smile and something very like a chuckle as he turned the end of the street and struck out across Golden Square towards his rooms in Conduit Street. The simple Frenchman, only half a rogue—even less than half—was now bamboozled and put aside as effectually as his cousin had been. Certainly there was a diamond, and an immense one; if only the Bouvier tradition were true, probably the famous "Mirror of Portugal"; and nothing stood between Dorrington and absolute possession of that diamond but an ordinary sort of case such as he dealt with every day. And he had made Bouvier pay a fee for the privilege of putting him completely on the track of it! Dorrington smiled again.

His dinner was spoilt by waiting, but he troubled little of that. He spread before him, and examined again, the pieces of glass and the cork. The bottle had been a druggist's ordinary flat bottle, graduated with dose-marks, and altogether seven inches high, or thereabout. It had, without a doubt, contained the chloroform wherewith Léon Bouvier had been assaulted, as Dorrington had judged from the smell of the cork. The fact of the bottle being corked showed that the chloroform had not been bought all at once—since in that case it would have been put up in a stoppered bottle. More probably it had been procured in very small quantities (ostensibly for toothache, or something of that kind) at different druggists, and put together in this larger bottle, which had originally been used for something else. The bottle had been distinguished by a label—the usual white label affixed by the druggist, with directions as to taking the medicine—and this label had been scraped off; all except a small piece at the bottom edge by the right hand side, whereon might be just distinguished the greater part of the letters N, E. The piece of glass that had lain a little way apart from the bottle was not a part of it, as a casual observer might have supposed. It was a fragment of a concave lens, with a channel ground in the edge.

III

At ten precisely next morning, as usual, Mr. Ludwig Hamer mounted the stairs of the house in Hatton Garden, wherein he rented half a room as office. He was a tall, fair man, wearing thick convex *pince-nez*. He spoke English like a native, and, indeed, he called himself an Englishman, though there were those who doubted the Briticism of his name. Scarce had he entered his office when Dorrington followed him.

The room had never been a very large one, and now a partition divided it in two, leaving a passage at one side only, by the window. On each side of this partition stood a small pedestal table, a couple of chairs, a copying-press, and the other articles usual in a meagrely furnished office. Dorrington strode past Bouvier's half of the room and came upon Hamer as he was hanging his coat on a peg. The letter of introduction had been burnt, since Dorrington had only asked for it in order to get Hamer's name and the Hatton Garden address without betraying to Bouvier the fact that he did not already know all about it.

"Good morning, Mr. Hamer," said Dorrington, loudly. "Sorry to see you're not well"—he pointed familiarly with his stick at a range of medicine bottles on the mantelpiece—"but it's very trying weather, of course. You've been suffering from toothache, I believe?"

Hamer seemed at first disposed to resent the loudness and familiarity of this speech, but at the reference to toothache he started suddenly and set his lips.

"Chloroform's a capital thing for toothache, Mr. Hamer, and for— for other things. I'm not in your line of business myself, but I believe it has even been used in the diamond trade."

"What do you mean?" asked Hamer, flushing angrily.

"Mean? Why, bless me—nothing more than I said. By the way, I'm afraid you dropped one of your medicine bottles last night. I've brought it back, though I'm afraid it's past repair. It's a good job you didn't quite clear the label off before you took it out with you, else I might have had a difficulty." Dorrington placed the fragments on the table. "You see you've just left the first letter of 'E.C.' in the druggist's address, and the last 'N' of Hatton Garden, just before it. There doesn't happen to be any other Garden in E.C. district that I know of, nor does the name of any other thoroughfare end in N—they are mostly streets, or lanes, or courts, you see. And there seems to be only one druggist in Hatton

Garden—capital fellow, no doubt—the one whose name and address I observe on those bottles on the mantelpiece."

Dorrington stood with his foot on a chair, and tapped his knee carelessly with his stick. Hamer dropped into the other chair and regarded him with a frown, though his face was pale. Presently he said, in a strained voice, "Well?"

"Yes; there *is* something else, Mr. Hamer, as you appear to suggest. I see you're wearing a new pair of glasses this morning; pity you broke the others last night, but I've brought the piece you left behind." He gathered up the broken bottle, and held up the piece of concave lens. "I think, after all, it's really best to use a cord with *pince-nez*. It's awkward, and it catches in things, I know, but it saves a breakage, and you're liable to get the glasses knocked off, you know—in certain circumstances."

Hamer sprang to his feet with a snarl, slammed the door, locked it, and turned on Dorrington. But now Dorrington had a revolver in his hand, though his manner was as genial as ever.

"Yes, yes," he said; "best to shut the door, of course. People listen, don't they? But sit down again. I'm not anxious to hurt you, and, as you will perceive, you're quite unable to hurt me. What I chiefly came to say is this: last evening my client, M. Léon Bouvier, of this office and the Café des Bons Camarades, was attacked in the passage adjoining his house by a man who was waiting for him, with a woman—was it really Mrs. Hamer? but there, I won't ask—keeping watch. He was robbed of a small old wooden box, containing charcoal and—a diamond. My name is Dorrington—firm of Dorrington & Hicks, which you may have heard of. That's my card. I've come to take away that diamond."

Hamer was pale and angry, but, in his way, was almost as calm as Dorrington. He put down the card without looking at it. "I don't understand you," he said. "How do you know I've got it?"

"Come, come, Mr. Hamer," Dorrington replied, rubbing the barrel of his revolver on his knee, "that's hardly worthy of you. You're a man of business, with a head on your shoulders—the sort of man I like doing business with, in fact. Men like ourselves needn't trifle. I've shown you most of the cards I hold, though not all, I assure you. I'll tell you, if you like, all about your little tour round among the druggists with the convenient toothache, all about the evenings on which you watched Bouvier home, and so on. But, really, need we, as men of the world, descend to such peddling detail?"

"Well, suppose I have got it, and suppose I refuse to give it you. What then?"

"What then? But why should we talk of unpleasant things? You won't refuse, you know."

"Do you mean you'd get it out of me by help of that pistol?"

"Well," said Dorrington, deliberately, "the pistol is noisy, and it makes a mess, and all that, but it's a useful thing, and I *might* do it with that, you know, in certain circumstances. But I wasn't thinking of it—there's a much less troublesome way."

"Which?"

"You're a slower man than I took you for, Mr. Hamer—or perhaps you haven't quite appreciated *me* yet. If I were to go to that window and call the police, what with the little bits of evidence in my pocket, and the other little bits that the druggists who sold the chloroform would give, and the other bits in reserve, that I prefer not to talk about just now—there would be rather an awkwardly complete case of robbery with violence, wouldn't there? And you'd have to lose the diamond after all, to say nothing of a little rest in gaol and general ruination."

"That sounds very well, but what about your client? Come now, you call me a man of the world, and I am one. How will your client account for the possession of a diamond worth eighty thousand pounds or so? He doesn't seem a millionaire. The police would want to know about him as well as about me, if you were such a fool as to bring them in. Where did *he* steal it, eh?"

Dorrington smiled and bowed at the question. "That's a very good card to play, Mr. Hamer," he said, "a capital card, really. To a superficial observer it might look like winning the trick. But I think I can trump it." He bent farther forward and tapped the table with the pistol-barrel. "Suppose I don't care one solitary dump what becomes of my client? Suppose I don't care whether he goes to gaol or stays out of it—in short, suppose I prefer my own interests to his?"

"Ho! ho!" Hamer cried. "I begin to understand. You want to grab the diamond for yourself then?"

"I haven't said anything of the kind, Mr. Hamer," Dorrington replied, suavely. "I have simply demanded the diamond which you stole last night, and I have mentioned an alternative."

"Oh, yes, yes, but we understand one another. Come, we'll arrange this. How much do you want?"

Dorrington stared at him stonily. "I—I beg your pardon," he said, "but I don't understand. I want the diamond you stole."

"But come now, we'll divide. Bouvier had no right to it, and he's out. You and I, perhaps, haven't much right to it, legally, but it's between us, and we're both in the same position."

"Pardon me," Dorrington replied, silkily, "but there you mistake. We are *not* in the same position, by a long way. You are liable to an instant criminal prosecution. I have simply come, authorised by my client, who bears all the responsibility, to demand a piece of property which you have stolen. That is the difference between our positions, Mr. Hamer. Come now, a policeman is just standing opposite. Shall I open the window and call him, or do you give in?"

"Oh, I give in, I suppose," Hamer groaned. "But you're a deal too hard. A man of your abilities shouldn't be so mean."

"That's right and reasonable," Dorrington answered briskly. "The wise man is the man who knows when he is beaten, and saves further trouble. You may not find me so mean after all, but I must have the stone first. I hold the trumps, and I'm not going to let the other player make conditions. Where's the diamond?"

"It isn't here—it's at home. You'll have to get it out of Mrs. Hamer. Shall I go and wire to her?"

"No, no," said Dorrington, "that's not the way. We'll just go together, and take Mrs. Hamer by surprise, I think. I mustn't let you out of sight, you know. Come, we'll get a hansom. Is it far?"

"Bessborough Street, Pimlico. You'll find Mrs. Hamer has a temper of her own."

"Well, well, we all have our failings. But before we start, now, observe." For a moment Dorrington was stern and menacing. "You wriggled a little at first, but that was quite natural. Now you've given in; and at the first sign of another wriggle I stop it once and for all. Understand? No tricks, now."

They entered a hansom at the door. Hamer was moody and silent at first, but under the influence of Dorrington's gay talk he opened out after a while. "Well," he said, "you're far the cleverest of the three, no doubt, and perhaps in that way you deserve to win. It's mighty smart for you to come in like this, and push Bouvier on one side and me on the other, and both of us helpless. But it's rough on me after having all the trouble."

"Don't be a bad loser, man!" Dorrington answered. "You might have had a deal more trouble and a deal more roughness too, I assure you."

"Oh yes, so I might. I'm not grumbling. But there's one thing has puzzled me all along. Where did Bouvier get that stone from?"

"He inherited it. It's the most important of the family jewels, I assure you."

"Oh, skittles! I might have known you wouldn't tell me, even if you knew yourself. But I should like to know. What sort of a duffer must it have been that let Bouvier do him for that big stone—Bouvier of all men in the world? Why, he was a record flat himself—couldn't tell a diamond from a glass marble, I should think. Why, he used to buy peddling little trays of rotters in the Garden at twice their value! And then he'd sell them for what he could get. I knew very well he wasn't going on systematically dropping money like that for no reason at all. He had some axe to grind, that was plain. And after a while he got asking timid questions as to the sale of big diamonds, and how it was done, and who bought them, and all that. That put me on it at once. All this buying and selling at a loss was a blind. He wanted to get into the trade to sell stolen diamonds, that was clear; and there was some value in them too, else he couldn't afford to waste months of time and lose money every day over it. So I kept my eye on him. I noticed, when he put his overcoat on, and thought I wasn't looking, he would settle a string of some sort round his neck, under his shirt-collar, and feel to pack up something close under his armpit. Then I just watched him home, and saw the sort of shanty he lived in. I mentioned these things to Mrs. H., and she was naturally indignant at the idea of a chap like Bouvier having something valuable in a dishonest way, and agreed with me that if possible it ought to be got from him, if only in the interests of virtue." Hamer laughed jerkily. "So at any rate we determined to get a look at whatever it was hanging round his neck, and we made the arrangements you know about. It seemed to me that Bouvier was pretty sure to lose it before long, one way or another, if it had any value at all, to judge by the way he was done in other matters. But I assure you I nearly fell down like Bouvier himself when I saw what it was. No wonder we left the bottle behind where I'd dropped it, after soaking the shawl—I wonder I didn't leave the shawl itself, and my hat, and everything. I assure you we sat up half last night looking at that wonderful stone!"

"No doubt. I shall have a good look at it myself, I assure you. Here is Bessborough Street. Which is the number?"

They alighted, and entered a house rather smaller than those about it. "Ask Mrs. Hamer to come here," said Hamer, gloomily, to the servant.

The men sat in the drawing-room. Presently Mrs. Hamer entered—a shortish, sharp, keen-eyed woman of forty-five. "This is Mr. Dorrington," said Hamer, "of Dorrington & Hicks, private detectives. He wants us to give him that diamond."

The little woman gave a sort of involuntary bounce, and exclaimed. "What? Diamond? What d'ye mean?"

"Oh, it's no good, Maria," Hamer answered dolefully. "I've tried it every way myself. One comfort is we're safe, as long as we give it up. Here," he added, turning to Dorrington, "show her some of your evidence—that'll convince her."

Very politely Dorrington brought forth, with full explanations, the cork and the broken glass; while Mrs. Hamer, biting hard at her thin lips, grew shinier and redder in the face every moment, and her hard gray eyes flashed fury.

"And you let this man," she burst out to her husband, when Dorrington had finished, "you let this man leave your office with these things in his possession after he had shown them to you, and you as big as he is, and bigger! Coward!"

"My dear, you don't appreciate Mr. Dorrington's forethought, hang it! I made preparations for the very line of action you recommend, but he was ready. He brought out a very well kept revolver, and he has it in his pocket now!"

Mrs. Hamer only glared, speechless with anger.

"You might just get Mr. Dorrington a whisky and soda, Maria," Hamer pursued, with a slight lift of the eyebrows which he did not intend Dorrington to see. The woman was on her feet in a moment.

"Thank you, no," interposed Dorrington, rising also, "I won't trouble you. I'd rather not drink anything just now, and, although I fear I may appear rude, I can't allow either of you to leave the room. In short," he added, "I must stay with you both till I get the diamond."

"And this man Bouvier," asked Mrs. Hamer, "what is his right to the stone?"

"Really, I don't feel competent to offer an opinion, do you know," Dorrington answered sweetly. "To tell the truth, M. Bouvier doesn't interest me very much."

"No go, Maria!" growled Hamer. "I've tried it all. The fact is we've got to give Dorrington the diamond. If we don't he'll just call in the police—then we shall lose diamond and everything else too. He doesn't care what becomes of Bouvier. He's got us, that's what it is. He won't even bargain to give us a share."

Mrs. Hamer looked quickly up. "Oh, but that's nonsense!" she said. "We've got the thing. We ought at least to say halves."

Her sharp eyes searched Dorrington's face, but there was no encouragement in it. "I am sorry to disappoint a lady," he said, "but this time it is my business to impose terms, not to submit to them. Come, the diamond!"

"Well, you'll give us something, surely?" the woman cried.

"Nothing is sure, madam, except that you will give me that diamond, or face a policeman in five minutes!"

The woman realised her helplessness. "Well," she said, "much good may it do you. You'll have to come and get it—I'm keeping it somewhere else. I'll go and get my hat."

Again Dorrington interposed. "I think we'll send your servant for the hat," he said, reaching for the bell-rope. "I'll come wherever you like, but I shall not leave you till this affair is settled, I promise you. And, as I reminded your husband a little time ago, you'll find tricks come expensive."

The servant brought Mrs. Hamer's hat and cloak, and that lady put them on, her eyes ablaze with anger. Dorrington made the pair walk before him to the front door, and followed them into the street. "Now," he said, "where is this place? Remember, no tricks!"

Mrs. Hamer turned towards Vauxhall Bridge. "It's just over by Upper Kennington Lane," she said. "Not far."

She paced out before them, Dorrington and Hamer following, the former affable and business-like, the latter apparently a little puzzled. When they came about the middle of the bridge, the woman turned suddenly. "Come, Mr. Dorrington," she said, in a more subdued voice than she had yet used, "I give in. It's no use trying to shake you off, I can see. I have the diamond with me. Here."

She put a little old black wooden box in his hand. He made to open the lid, which fitted tightly, and at that moment the woman, pulling her other hand free from under her cloak, flung away over the parapet something that shone like fifty points of electric light.

"There it goes!" she screamed aloud, pointing with her finger. "There's your diamond, you dirty thief! You bully! Go after it now, you spy!"

The great diamond made a curve of glitter and disappeared into the river.

For the moment Dorrington lost his cool temper. He seized the woman by the arm. "Do you know what you've done, you wild cat?" he exclaimed.

"Yes, I do!" the woman screamed, almost foaming with passion, while boys began to collect, though there had been but few people on the bridge. "Yes, I do! And now you can do what you please, you thief! you bully!"

Dorrington was calm again in a moment. He shrugged his shoulders and turned away. Hamer was frightened. He came at Dorrington's side and faltered, "I—I told you she had a temper. What will you do?"

Dorrington forced a laugh. "Oh, nothing," he said. "What can I do? Locking you up now wouldn't fetch the diamond back. And besides I'm not sure that Mrs. Hamer won't attend to your punishment faithfully enough." And he walked briskly away.

"What did she do, Bill?" asked one boy of another.

"Why, didn't ye see? She chucked that man's watch in the river."

"Garn! that wasn't his watch!" interrupted a third, "it was a little glass tumbler. I see it!"

"HAVE YOU GOT MY DIAMOND?" asked the agonised Léon Bouvier of Dorrington a day later.

"No, I have not," Dorrington replied drily. "Nor has your cousin Jacques. But I know where it is, and you can get it as easily as I."

"*Mon Dieu!* Where?"

"At the bottom of the river Thames, exactly in the centre, rather to the right of Vauxhall Bridge, looking from this side. I expect it will be rediscovered in some future age, when the bed of the Thames is a diamond field."

The rest of Bouvier's savings went in the purchase of a boat, and in this, with a pail on a long rope, he was very busy for some time afterward. But he only got a great deal of mud into his boat.

IV

THE AFFAIR OF THE "AVALANCHE BICYCLE
AND TYRE CO., LIMITED"

I

CYCLE COMPANIES WERE IN THE market everywhere. Immense
fortunes were being made in a few days and sometimes little fortunes
were being lost to build them up. Mining shares were dull for a season,
and any company with the word "cycle" or "tyre" in its title was certain
to attract capital, no matter what its prospects were like in the eyes of the
expert. All the old private cycle companies suddenly were offered to the
public, and their proprietors, already rich men, built themselves houses
on the Riviera, bought yachts, ran racehorses, and left business for
ever. Sometimes the shareholders got their money's worth, sometimes
more, sometimes less—sometimes they got nothing but total loss; but
still the game went on. One could never open a newspaper without
finding, displayed at large, the prospectus of yet another cycle company
with capital expressed in six figures at least, often in seven. Solemn
old dailies, into whose editorial heads no new thing ever found its
way till years after it had been forgotten elsewhere, suddenly exhibited
the scandalous phenomenon of "broken columns" in their advertising
sections, and the universal prospectuses stretched outrageously across
half or even all the page—a thing to cause apoplexy in the bodily system
of any self-respecting manager of the old school.

In the midst of this excitement it chanced that the firm of Dorrington
& Hicks were engaged upon an investigation for the famous and
long-established "Indestructible Bicycle and Tricycle Manufacturing
Company," of London and Coventry. The matter was not one of sufficient
intricacy or difficulty to engage Dorrington's personal attention, and it
was given to an assistant. There was some doubt as to the validity of a
certain patent having reference to a particular method of tightening the
spokes and truing the wheels of a bicycle, and Dorrington's assistant
had to make inquiries (without attracting attention to the matter) as
to whether or not there existed any evidence, either documentary or in
the memory of veterans, of the use of this method, or anything like it,

before the year 1885. The assistant completed his inquiries and made his report to Dorrington. Now I think I have said that, from every evidence I have seen, the chief matter of Dorrington's solicitude was his own interest, and just at this time he had heard, as had others, much of the money being made in cycle companies. Also, like others, he had conceived a great desire to get the confidential advice of somebody "in the know"—advice which might lead him into the "good thing" desired by all the greedy who flutter about at the outside edge of the stock and share market. For this reason Dorrington determined to make this small matter of the wheel patent an affair of personal report. He was a man of infinite resource, plausibility and good-companionship, and there was money going in the cycle trade. Why then should he lose an opportunity of making himself pleasant in the inner groves of that trade, and catch whatever might come his way—information, syndicate shares, directorships, anything? So that Dorrington made himself master of his assistant's information, and proceeded to the head office of the "Indestructible" company on Holborn Viaduct, resolved to become the entertaining acquaintance of the managing director.

On his way his attention was attracted by a very elaborately fitted cycle shop, which his recollection told him was new. "The Avalanche Bicycle and Tyre Company" was the legend gilt above the great plate-glass window, and in the window itself stood many brilliantly enamelled and plated bicycles, each labelled on the frame with the flaming red and gold transfer of the firm; and in the midst of all was another bicycle covered with dried mud, of which, however, sufficient had been carefully cleared away to expose a similar glaring transfer to those that decorated the rest—with a placard announcing that on this particular machine somebody had ridden some incredible distance on bad roads in very little more than no time at all. A crowd stood about the window and gaped respectfully at the placard, the bicycles, the transfers, and the mud, though they paid little attention to certain piles of folded white papers, endorsed in bold letters with the name of the company, with the suffix "limited" and the word "prospectus" in bloated black letter below. These, however, Dorrington observed at once, for he had himself that morning, in common with several thousand other people, received one by post. Also half a page of his morning paper had been filled with a copy of that same prospectus, and the afternoon had brought another copy in the evening paper. In the list of directors there was a titled name or two, together with a few unknown names—doubtless the "practical men." And below this list there were such positive promises of tremendous dividends, backed up and proved beyond dispute by such ingenious piles of business-like figures, every line of figures referring to some other line for testimonials to its perfect genuineness and accuracy, that any reasonable man, it would seem, must instantly sell the hat off his head and the boots off his feet to buy one share at least, and so make his fortune for ever. True, the business was but lately established, but that was just it. It had rushed ahead with such amazing rapidity (as was natural with an avalanche) that it had got altogether out of hand, and orders couldn't be executed at all; wherefore the proprietors were reluctantly compelled to let the public have some of the luck. This was Thursday. The share list was to be opened on Monday morning and closed inexorably at four o'clock on Tuesday afternoon, with a merciful extension to Wednesday morning for the candidates for wealth who were so unfortunate as to live in the country. So that it behoved everybody to waste no time lest he be numbered among the unlucky whose subscription-money should be returned in full, failing allotment. The prospectus did not absolutely say it in so many words, but no rational person could fail to feel that the directors were fervently hoping that nobody would get injured in the rush.

Dorrington passed on and reached the well-known establishment of the "Indestructible Bicycle Company." This was already a limited company of a private sort, and had been so for ten years or more. And before that the concern had had eight or nine years of prosperous experience. The founder of the firm, Mr. Paul Mallows, was now the managing director, and a great pillar of the cycling industry. Dorrington gave a clerk his card, and asked to see Mr. Mallows.

Mr. Mallows was out, it seemed, but Mr. Stedman, the secretary, was in, and him Dorrington saw. Mr. Stedman was a pleasant, youngish man, who had been a famous amateur bicyclist in his time, and was still an enthusiast. In ten minutes business was settled and dismissed, and Dorrington's tact had brought the secretary into a pleasant discursive chat, with much exchange of anecdote. Dorrington expressed much interest in the subject of bicycling, and, seeing that Stedman had been a racing man, particularly as to bicycling races.

"There'll be a rare good race on Saturday, I expect," Stedman said. "Or rather," he went on, "I expect the fifty miles record will go. I fancy our man Gillett is pretty safe to win, but he'll have to move, and I quite expect to see a good set of new records on our advertisements next week.

The next best man is Lant—the new fellow, you know—who rides for the 'Avalanche' people."

"Let's see, they're going to the public as a limited company, aren't they?" Dorrington asked casually.

Stedman nodded, with a little grimace.

"You don't think it's a good thing, perhaps," Dorrington said, noticing the grimace. "Is that so?"

"Well," Stedman answered, "of course I can't say. I don't know much about the firm—nobody does, as far as I can tell—but they seem to have got a business together in almost no time; that is, if the business is as genuine as it looks at first sight. But they want a rare lot of capital, and then the prospectus—well, I've seen more satisfactory ones, you know. I don't say it isn't all right, of course, but still I shan't go out of my way to recommend any friends of mine to plunge on it."

"You won't?"

"No, I won't. Though no doubt they'll get their capital, or most of it. Almost any cycle or tyre company can get subscribed just now. And this 'Avalanche' affair is both, and it is so well advertised, you know. Lant has been winning on their mounts just lately, and they've been booming it for all they're worth. By Jove, if they could only screw him up to win the fifty miles on Saturday, and beat our man Gillett, that *would* give them a push! Just at the correct moment too. Gillett's never been beaten yet at the distance, you know. But Lant can't do it—though, as I have said, he'll make some fast riding—it'll be a race, I tell you!"

"I should like to see it."

"Why not come? See about it, will you? And perhaps you'd like to run down to the track after dinner this evening and see our man training— awfully interesting, I can tell you, with all the pacing machinery and that. Will you come?"

Dorrington expressed himself delighted, and suggested that Stedman should dine with him before going to the track. Stedman, for his part, charmed with his new acquaintance—as everybody was at a first meeting with Dorrington—assented gladly.

At that moment the door of Stedman's room was pushed open and a well-dressed, middle-aged man, with a shaven, flabby face, appeared. "I beg pardon," he said, "I thought you were alone. I've just ripped my finger against the handle of my brougham door as I came in—the screw sticks out. Have you a piece of sticking plaster?" He extended a bleeding finger as he spoke. Stedman looked doubtfully at his desk.

"Here is some court plaster," Dorrington exclaimed, producing his pocket-book. "I always carry it—it's handier than ordinary sticking plaster. How much do you want?"

"Thanks—an inch or so."

"This is Mr. Dorrington, of Messrs. Dorrington & Hicks, Mr. Mallows," Stedman said. "Our managing director, Mr. Paul Mallows, Mr. Dorrington."

Dorrington was delighted to make Mr. Mallows's acquaintance, and he busied himself with a careful strapping of the damaged finger. Mr. Mallows had the large frame of a man of strong build who has had much hard bodily work, but there hung about it the heavier, softer flesh that told of a later period of ease and sloth. "Ah, Mr. Mallows," Stedman said, "the bicycle's the safest thing, after all! Dangerous things these broughams!"

"Ah, you younger men," Mr. Mallows replied, with a slow and rounded enunciation, "you younger men can afford to be active. We elders—"

"Can afford a brougham," Dorrington added, before the managing director began the next word. "Just so—and the bicycle does it all; wonderful thing the bicycle!"

Dorrington had not misjudged his man, and the oblique reference to his wealth flattered Mr. Mallows. Dorrington went once more through his report as to the spoke patent, and then Mr. Mallows bade him good-bye.

"Good-day, Mr. Dorrington, good-day," he said. "I am extremely obliged by your careful personal attention to this matter of the patent. We may leave it with Mr. Stedman now, I think. Good-day. I hope soon to have the pleasure of meeting you again." And with clumsy stateliness Mr. Mallows vanished.

II

"SO YOU DON'T THINK THE 'Avalanche' good business as an investment?" Dorrington said once more as he and Stedman, after an excellent dinner, were cabbing it to the track.

"No, no," Stedman answered, "don't touch it! There's better things than that coming along presently. Perhaps I shall be able to put you in for something, you know, a bit later; but don't be in a hurry. As to the 'Avalanche,' even if everything else were satisfactory, there's too much 'booming' being done just now to please me. All sorts of rumours, you know, of their having something 'up their sleeve,' and so on; mysterious hints in the papers, and all that, as to something revolutionary being in hand with the 'Avalanche' people. Perhaps there is. But why they don't fetch it out in view of the public subscription for shares is more than I can understand, unless they don't want too much of a rush. And as to that, well they don't look like modestly shrinking from anything of that sort up to the present."

They were at the track soon after seven o'clock, but Gillett was not yet riding. Dorrington remarked that Gillett appeared to begin late.

"Well," Stedman explained, "he's one of those fellows that afternoon training doesn't seem to suit, unless it is a bit of walking exercise. He just does a few miles in the morning and a spurt or two, and then he comes on just before sunset for a fast ten or fifteen miles—that is, when he is getting fit for such a race as Saturday's. To-night will be his last spin of that length before Saturday, because to-morrow will be the day before the race. To-morrow he'll only go a spurt or two, and rest most of the day."

They strolled about inside the track, the two highly "banked" ends whereof seemed to a nearsighted person in the centre to be solid erect walls, along the face of which the training riders skimmed, fly-fashion. Only three or four persons beside themselves were in the enclosure when they first came, but in ten minutes' time Mr. Paul Mallows came across the track.

"Why," said Stedman to Dorrington, "here's the Governor! It isn't often he comes down here. But I expect he's anxious to see how Gillett's going, in view of Saturday."

"Good evening, Mr. Mallows," said Dorrington. "I hope the finger's all right? Want any more plaster?"

"Good evening, good evening," responded Mr. Mallows heavily. "Thank you, the finger's not troubling me a bit." He held it up, still decorated by the black plaster. "Your plaster remains, you see—I was a little careful not to fray it too much in washing, that was all." And Mr. Mallows sat down on a light iron garden-chair (of which several stood here and there in the enclosure) and began to watch the riding.

The track was clear, and dusk was approaching when at last the great Gillett made his appearance on the track. He answered a friendly question or two put to him by Mallows and Stedman, and then, giving his coat to his trainer, swung off along the track on his bicycle, led in front by a tandem and closely attended by a triplet. In fifty yards his pace quickened, and he settled down into a swift even pace, regular as clockwork. Sometimes the tandem and sometimes the triplet went to the front, but Gillett neither checked nor heeded as, nursed by his pacers, who were directed by the trainer from the centre, he swept along mile after mile, each mile in but a few seconds over the two minutes.

"Look at the action!" exclaimed Stedman with enthusiasm. "Just watch him. Not an ounce of power wasted there! Did you ever see more regular ankle work? And did anybody ever sit a machine quite so well as that? Show me a movement anywhere above the hips!"

"Ah," said Mr. Mallows, "Gillett has a wonderful style—a wonderful style, really!"

The men in the enclosure wandered about here and there on the grass, watching Gillett's riding as one watches the performance of a great piece of art—which, indeed, was what Gillett's riding was. There were, besides Mallows, Stedman, Dorrington and the trainer, two officials of the Cyclists' Union, an amateur racing man named Sparks, the track superintendent and another man. The sky grew darker, and gloom fell about the track. The machines became invisible, and little could be seen of the riders across the ground but the row of rhythmically working legs and the white cap that Gillett wore. The trainer had just told Stedman that there would be three fast laps and then his man would come off the track.

"Well, Mr. Stedman," said Mr. Mallows, "I think we shall be all right for Saturday."

"Rather!" answered Stedman confidently. "Gillett's going great guns, and steady as a watch!"

The pace now suddenly increased. The tandem shot once more to the front, the triplet hung on the rider's flank, and the group of swishing wheels flew round the track at a "one-fifty" gait. The spectators turned about, following the riders round the track with their eyes. And then, swinging into the straight from the top bend, the tandem checked suddenly and gave a little jump. Gillett crashed into it from behind, and the triplet, failing to clear, wavered and swung, and crashed over and along the track too. All three machines and six men were involved in one complicated smash.

Everybody rushed across the grass, the trainer first. Then the cause of the disaster was seen. Lying on its side on the track, with men and bicycles piled over and against it, was one of the green painted light iron garden-chairs that had been standing in the enclosure. The triplet men were struggling to their feet, and though much cut and shaken, seemed the least hurt of the lot. One of the men of the tandem was insensible, and Gillett, who from his position had got all the worst of it, lay senseless too, badly cut and bruised, and his left arm was broken.

The trainer was cursing and tearing his hair. "If I knew who'd done this," Stedman cried, "I'd *pulp* him with that chair!"

"Oh, that betting, that betting!" wailed Mr. Mallows, hopping about distractedly; "see what it leads people into doing! It can't have been an accident, can it?"

"Accident? Skittles! A man doesn't put a chair on a track in the dark and leave it there by accident. Is anybody getting away there from the outside of the track?"

"No, there's nobody. He wouldn't wait till this; he's clear off a minute ago and more. Here, Fielders! Shut the outer gate, and we'll see who's about."

But there seemed to be no suspicious character. Indeed, except for the ground-man, his boy, Gillett's trainer, and a racing man, who had just finished dressing in the pavilion, there seemed to be nobody about beyond those whom everybody had seen standing in the enclosure. But there had been ample time for anybody, standing unnoticed at the outer rails, to get across the track in the dark, just after the riders had passed, place the obstruction, and escape before the completion of the lap.

The damaged men were helped or carried into the pavilion, and the damaged machines were dragged after them. "I will give fifty pounds gladly—more, a hundred," said Mr. Mallows, excitedly, "to anybody who will find out who put that chair on the track. It might have ended in murder. Some wretched bookmaker, I suppose, who has taken too many bets on Gillett. As I've said a thousand times, betting is the curse of all sport nowadays."

"The governor excites himself a great deal about betting and bookmakers," Stedman said to Dorrington, as they walked toward the pavilion, "but, between you and me, I believe some of the 'Avalanche' people are in this. The betting bee is always in Mallows's bonnet, but as a matter of fact there's very little betting at all on cycle races, and what there is is little more than a matter of half-crowns or at most half-sovereigns on the day of the race. No bookmaker ever makes a heavy book first. Still there *may* be something in it this time, of course. But look at the 'Avalanche' people. With Gillett away their man can certainly win on Saturday, and if only the weather keeps fair he can almost as certainly beat the record; just at present the fifty miles is fairly easy, and it's bound to go soon. Indeed, our intention was that Gillett should pull it down on Saturday. He was a safe winner, bar accidents, and it was good odds on his altering the record, if the weather were any good at all. With Gillett out of it Lant is just about as certain a winner as our man would be if all were well. And there would be a boom for the 'Avalanche' company, on the very eve of the share subscription! Lant, you must know, was very second-rate till this season, but he has improved wonderfully in the last month or two, since he has been with the 'Avalanche' people. Let him win, and they can point to the machine as responsible for it all. 'Here,' they will say in effect, 'is a man who could rarely get in front, even in second-class company, till he rode an 'Avalanche.' Now he beats the world's record for fifty miles on it, and makes rings round the topmost professionals!' Why, it will be worth thousands of capital to them. Of course the subscription of capital won't hurt us, but the loss of the record may, and to have Gillett knocked out like this in the middle of the season is serious."

"Yes, I suppose with you it is more than a matter of this one race."

"Of course. And so it will be with the 'Avalanche' company. Don't you see, with Gillett probably useless for the rest of the season, Lant will have it all his own way at anything over ten miles. That'll help to boom up the shares and there'll be big profit made on trading in them. Oh, I tell you this thing seems pretty suspicious to me."

"Look here," said Dorrington, "can you borrow a light for me, and let me run over with it to the spot where the smash took place? The people have cleared into the pavilion, and I could go alone."

"Certainly. Will you have a try for the governor's hundred?"

"Well, perhaps. But anyway there's no harm in doing you a good turn if I can, while I'm here. Some day perhaps you'll do me one."

"Right you are—I'll ask Fielders, the ground-man."

A lantern was brought, and Dorrington betook himself to the spot where the iron chair still lay, while Stedman joined the rest of the crowd in the pavilion.

Dorrington minutely examined the grass within two yards of the place where the chair lay, and then, crossing the track and getting over the rails, did the same with the damp gravel that paved the outer ring. The track itself was of cement, and unimpressionable by footmarks, but nevertheless he scrutinised that with equal care, as well as the rails.

Then he turned his attention to the chair. It was, as I have said, a light chair made of flat iron strip, bent to shape and riveted. It had seen good service, and its present coat of green paint was evidently far from being its original one. Also it was rusty in places, and parts had been repaired and strengthened with cross-pieces secured by bolts and square nuts, some rusty and loose. It was from one of these square nuts, holding a cross-piece that stayed the back at the top, that Dorrington secured some object—it might have been a hair—which he carefully transferred to his pocket-book. This done, with one more glance round, he betook himself to the pavilion.

A surgeon had arrived, and he reported well of the chief patient. It was a simple fracture, and a healthy subject. When Dorrington entered, preparations were beginning for setting the limb. There was a sofa in the pavilion, and the surgeon saw no reason for removing the patient till all was made secure.

"Found anything?" asked Stedman in a low tone of Dorrington.

Dorrington shook his head. "Not much," he answered at a whisper. "I'll think over it later."

Dorrington asked one of the Cyclists' Union officials for the loan of a pencil, and, having made a note with it, immediately, in another part of the room, asked Sparks, the amateur, to lend him another.

Stedman had told Mr. Mallows of Dorrington's late employment with the lantern, and the managing director now said quietly, "You remember what I said about rewarding anybody who discovered the perpetrator of this outrage, Mr. Dorrington? Well, I was excited at the time, but I quite hold to it. It is a shameful thing. You have been looking about the grounds, I hear. I hope you have come across something that will enable you to find something out. Nothing will please me more than to have to pay you, I'm sure."

"Well," Dorrington confessed, "I'm afraid I haven't seen anything very big in the way of a clue, Mr. Mallows; but I'll think a bit. The worst of it is, you never know who these betting men are, do you, once they get away? There are so many, and it may be anybody. Not only that, but they may bribe anybody."

"Yes, of course—there's no end to their wickedness, I'm afraid. Stedman suggests that trade rivalry may have had something to do with it. But that seems an uncharitable view, don't you think? Of course we stand very high, and there are jealousies and all that, but this is a thing I'm sure no firm would think of stooping to, for a moment. No, it's betting that is at the bottom of this, I fear. And I hope, Mr. Dorrington, that you will make some attempt to find the guilty parties."

Presently Stedman spoke to Dorrington again. "Here's something that may help you," he said. "To begin with, it must have been done by some one from the outside of the track."

"Why?"

"Well, at least every probability's that way. Everybody inside was directly interested in Gillett's success, excepting the Union officials and Sparks, who's a gentleman and quite above suspicion, as much so, indeed, as the Union officials. Of course there was the ground-man, but he's all right, I'm sure."

"And the trainer?"

"Oh, that's altogether improbable—altogether. I was going to say—"

"And there's that other man who was standing about; I haven't heard who he was."

"Right you are. I don't know him either. Where is he now?"

But the man had gone.

"Look here, I'll make some quiet inquiries about that man," Stedman pursued. "I forgot all about him in the excitement of the moment. I was going to say that although whoever did it could easily have got away by the gate before the smash came, he might not have liked to go that way in case of observation in passing the pavilion. In that case he could have got away (and indeed he could have got into the grounds to begin with) by way of one of those garden walls that bound the ground just by where the smash occurred. If that were so he must either live in one of the houses, or he must know somebody that does. Perhaps you might put a man to smell about along that road—it's only a short one; Chisnall Road's the name."

"Yes, yes," Dorrington responded patiently. "There might be something in that."

By this time Gillett's arm was in a starched bandage and secured by splints, and a cab was ready to take him home. Mr. Mallows took Stedman away with him, expressing a desire to talk business, and Dorrington went home by himself. He did not turn down Chisnall Road. But he walked jauntily along toward the nearest cab-stand, and once or twice he chuckled, for he saw his way to a delightfully lucrative financial operation in cycle companies, without risk of capital.

The cab gained, he called at the lodgings of two of his men assistants and gave them instant instructions. Then he packed a small bag at his rooms in Conduit Street, and at midnight was in the late fast train for Birmingham.

III

THE PROSPECTUS OF THE "AVALANCHE Bicycle and Tyre Company" stated that the works were at Exeter and Birmingham. Exeter is a delightful old town, but it can scarcely be regarded as the centre of the cycle trade; neither is it in especially easy and short communication with Birmingham. It was the sort of thing that any critic anxious to pick holes in the prospectus might wonder at, and so one of Dorrington's assistants had gone by the night mail to inspect the works. It was from this man that Dorrington, in Birmingham, about noon on the day after Gillett's disaster, received this telegram—

> *Works here old disused cloth-mills just out of town. Closed and empty but with big new signboard and notice that works now running are at Birmingham. Agent says only deposit paid— tenancy agreement not signed.*
>
> *Farrish*

The telegram increased Dorrington's satisfaction, for he had just taken a look at the Birmingham works. They were not empty, though nearly so, nor were they large; and a man there had told him that the chief premises, where most of the work was done, were at Exeter. And the hollower the business the better prize he saw in store for himself. He had already, early in the morning, indulged in a telegram on his own account, though he had not signed it. This was how it ran—

> *Mallows, 58, Upper Sandown Place,*
> *London, W.*
> *Fear all not safe here. Run down by 10.10 train without fail.*

Thus it happened that at a little later than half-past eight Dorrington's other assistant, watching the door of No. 58, Upper Sandown Place, saw a telegram delivered, and immediately afterward Mr. Paul Mallows in much haste dashed away in a cab which was called from the end of the street. The assistant followed in another. Mr. Mallows dismissed his cab at a theatrical wig-maker's in Bow Street and entered. When he emerged in little more than forty minutes' time, none but a practised watcher, who had guessed the reason of the visit, would have recognised him. He had not assumed the clumsy disguise of a false beard. He was "made up" deftly. His colour was heightened, and his face seemed thinner. There was no heavy accession of false hair, but a slight crêpe-hair whisker at each side made a better and less pronounced disguise. He seemed a younger, healthier man. The watcher saw him safely off to Birmingham by the ten minutes past ten train, and then gave Dorrington note by telegraph of the guise in which Mr. Mallows was travelling.

Now this train was timed to arrive at Birmingham at one, which was the reason that Dorrington had named it in the anonymous telegram. The entrance to the "Avalanche" works was by a large gate, which was closed, but which was provided with a small door to pass a man. Within was a yard, and at a little before one o'clock Dorrington pushed open the small door, peeped, and entered. Nobody was about in the yard, and what little noise could be heard came from a particular part of the building on the right. A pile of solid "export" crates stood to the left, and these Dorrington had noted at his previous call that morning as making a suitable hiding-place for temporary use. Now he slipped behind them and awaited the stroke of one. Prompt at the hour a door on the opposite side of the yard swung open, and two men and a boy emerged and climbed one after another through the little door in the big gate. Then presently another man, not a workman, but apparently a sort of overseer, came from the opposite door, which he carelessly let fall-to behind him, and he also disappeared through the little door, which he then locked. Dorrington was now alone in the sole active works of the "Avalanche Bicycle and Tyre Company, Limited."

He tried the door opposite and found it was free to open. Within he saw in a dark corner a candle which had been left burning, and opposite him a large iron enamelling oven, like an immense safe, and round about, on benches, were strewn heaps of the glaring red and gold transfer which Dorrington had observed the day before on the machines exhibited in the Holborn Viaduct window. Some of the frames had the label newly applied, and others were still plain. It would seem that the chief business of the "Avalanche Bicycle and Tyre Company, Limited," was the attaching of labels to previously nondescript machines. But there was little time to examine further, and indeed Dorrington presently heard the noise of a key in the outer gate. So he stood and waited by the enamelling oven to welcome Mr. Mallows.

As the door was pushed open Dorrington advanced and bowed politely. Mallows started guiltily, but, remembering his disguise, steadied himself, and asked gruffly, "Well, sir, and who are you?"

"I," answered Dorrington with perfect composure, "I am Mr. Paul Mallows—you may have heard of me in connection with the 'Indestructible Bicycle Company.'"

Mallows was altogether taken aback. But then it struck him that perhaps the detective, anxious to win the reward he had offered in the matter of the Gillett outrage, was here making inquiries in the assumed character of the man who stood, impenetrably disguised, before him. So after a pause he asked again, a little less gruffly, "And what may be your business?"

"Well," said Dorrington, "I did think of taking shares in this company. I suppose there would be no objection to the managing director of another company taking shares in this?"

"No," answered Mallows, wondering what all this was to lead to.

"Of course not; I'm sure *you* don't think so, eh?" Dorrington, as he spoke, looked in the other's face with a sly leer, and Mallows began to feel altogether uncomfortable. "But there's one other thing," Dorrington pursued, taking out his pocket-book, though still maintaining his leer in Mallows's face—"one other thing. And by the way, *will* you have another piece of court plaster now I've got it out? Don't say no. It's a pleasure to oblige you, really." And Dorrington, his leer growing positively fiendish, tapped the side of his nose with the case of court plaster.

Mallows paled under the paint, gasped, and felt for support. Dorrington laughed pleasantly. "Come, come," he said, "don't be frightened. I admire your cleverness, Mr. Mallows, and I shall arrange everything pleasantly, as you will see. And as to the court plaster, if you'd rather not have it you needn't. You have another piece on now, I see. Why didn't you get them to paint it over at Clarkson's? They really did the face very well, though! And there again you were quite right. Such a man as yourself was likely to be recognised in such a place as Birmingham, and that would have been unfortunate for both of us— *both* of us, I assure you. . . Man alive, don't look as though I was going to cut your throat! I'm not, I assure you. You're a smart man of business, and I happen to have spotted a little operation of yours, that's all. I shall arrange easy terms for you. . . Pull yourself together and talk business before the men come back. Here, sit on this bench."

Mallows, staring amazedly in Dorrington's face, suffered himself to be led to a bench, and sat on it.

"Now," said Dorrington, "the first thing is a little matter of a hundred pounds. That was the reward you promised if I should discover who broke Gillett's arm last night. Well, I *have*. Do you happen to have any notes with you? If not, make it a cheque."

"But—but—how—I mean who—who—"

"Tut, tut! Don't waste time, Mr. Mallows. *Who?* Why, yourself, of course. I knew all about it before I left you last night, though it wasn't quite convenient to claim the reward then, for reasons you'll understand presently. Come, that little hundred!"

"But what—what proof have you? I'm not to be bounced like this, you know." Mr. Mallows was gathering his faculties again.

"Proof? Why, man alive, be reasonable! Suppose I have none—none at all? What difference does that make? Am I to walk out and tell your fellow directors where I have met you—here—or am I to have that hundred? More, am I to publish abroad that Mr. Paul Mallows is the moving spirit in the rotten 'Avalanche Bicycle Company'?"

"Well," Mallows answered reluctantly, "if you put it like that—"

"But I only put it like that to make you see things reasonably. As a matter of fact your connection with this new company is enough to bring your little performance with the iron chair pretty near proof. But I got at it from the other side. See here—you're much too clumsy with your fingers, Mr. Mallows. First you go and tear the tip of your middle finger opening your brougham door, and have to get court plaster from me. Then you let that court plaster get frayed at the edge, and you still keep it on. After that you execute your very successful chair operation. When the eyes of the others are following the bicycles you take the chair in the hand with the plaster on it, catching hold of it at the place where a rough, loose, square nut protrudes, and you pitch it on to the track so clumsily and nervously that the nut carries away the frayed thread of the court plaster with it. Here it is, you see, still in my pocket-book, where I put it last night by the light of the lantern; just a sticky black silk thread, that's all. I've only brought it to show you I'm playing a fair game with you. Of course I might easily have got a witness before I took the thread off the nut, if I had thought you were likely to fight the matter. But I knew you were not. You can't fight, you know, with this bogus company business known to me. So that I am only showing you this thread as an act of grace, to prove that I have stumped you with perfect fairness. And now the hundred. Here's a fountain pen, if you want one."

"Well," said Mallows glumly, "I suppose I must, then." He took the pen and wrote the cheque. Dorrington blotted it on the pad of his pocket-book and folded it away.

"So much for that!" he said. "That's just a little preliminary, you understand. We've done these little things just as a guarantee of good faith—not necessarily for publication, though you must remember that as yet there's nothing to prevent it. I've done you a turn by finding out who upset those bicycles, as you so ardently wished me to do last night, and you've loyally fulfilled your part of the contract by paying the promised reward—though I must say that you haven't paid with all the delight and pleasure you spoke of at the time. But I'll forgive you that, and now that the little *hors d'oeuvre* is disposed of, we'll proceed to serious business."

Mallows looked uncomfortably glum.

"But you mustn't look so ashamed of yourself, you know," Dorrington said, purposely misinterpreting his glumness. "It's all business. You were disposed for a little side flutter, so to speak—a little speculation outside your regular business. Well, you mustn't be ashamed of that."

"No," Mallows observed, assuming something of his ordinarily ponderous manner; "no, of course not. It's a little speculative deal. Everybody does it, and there's a deal of money going."

"Precisely. And since everybody does it, and there is so much money going, you are only making your share."

"Of course." Mr. Mallows was almost pompous by now.

"*Of* course." Dorrington coughed slightly. "Well now, do you know, I am exactly the same sort of man as yourself—if you don't mind the comparison. *I* am disposed for a little side flutter, so to speak—a little speculation outside my regular business. I also am not ashamed of it. And since everybody does it, and there is so much money going—why, *I* am thinking of making *my* share. So we are evidently a pair, and naturally intended for each other!"

Mr. Paul Mallows here looked a little doubtful.

"See here, now," Dorrington proceeded. "I have lately taken it into my head to operate a little on the cycle share market. That was why I came round myself about that little spoke affair, instead of sending an assistant. I wanted to know somebody who understood the cycle trade, from whom I might get tips. You see I'm perfectly frank with you. Well,

I have succeeded uncommonly well. And I want you to understand that I have gone every step of the way by fair work. I took nothing for granted, and I played the game fairly. When you asked me (as you had anxious reason to ask) if I had found anything, I told you there was nothing very big—and see what a little thing the thread was! Before I came away from the pavilion I made sure that you were really the only man there with black court plaster on his fingers. I had noticed the hands of every man but two, and I made an excuse of borrowing something to see those. I saw your thin pretence of suspecting the betting men, and I played up to it. I have had a telegraphic report on your Exeter works this morning—a deserted cloth mills with nothing on it of yours but a signboard, and only a deposit of rent paid. *There* they referred to the works here. *Here* they referred to the works there. It was very clever, really! Also I have had a telegraphic report of your make-up adventure this morning. Clarkson does it marvellously, doesn't he? And, by the way, that telegram bringing you down to Birmingham was not from your confederate here, as perhaps you fancied. It was from me. Thanks for coming so promptly. I managed to get a quiet look round here just before you arrived, and on the whole the conclusion I come to as to the 'Avalanche Bicycle and Tyre Company, Limited,' is this: A clever man, whom it gives me great pleasure to know," with a bow to Mallows, "conceives the notion of offering the public the very rottenest cycle company ever planned, and all without appearing in it himself. He finds what little capital is required; his two or three confederates help to make up a board of directors, with one or two titled guinea-pigs, who know nothing of the company and care nothing, and the rest's easy. A professional racing man is employed to win races and make records, on machines which have been specially made by another firm (perhaps it was the 'Indestructible,' who knows?) to a private order, and afterwards decorated with the name and style of the bogus company on a transfer. For ordinary sale, bicycles of the 'trade' description are bought—so much a hundred from the factors, and put your own name on 'em. They come cheap, and they sell at a good price—the profit pays all expenses and perhaps a bit over; and by the time they all break down the company will be successfully floated, the money—the capital—will be divided, the moving spirit and his confederates will have disappeared, and the guinea-pigs will be left to stand the racket—if there is a racket. And the moving spirit will remain unsuspected, a man of account in the trade all the time! Admirable! All the work to be done at the 'works' is the sticking on of labels and a bit of enamelling. Excellent, all round! Isn't that about the size of your operations?"

"Well, yes," Mallows answered, a little reluctantly, but with something of modest pride in his manner, "that was the notion, since you speak so plainly."

"And it shall be the notion. All—everything—shall be as you have planned it, with one exception, which is this. The moving spirit shall divide his plunder with me."

"*You?* But—but—why, I gave you a hundred just now!"

"Dear, dear! Why will you harp so much on that vulgar little hundred? That's settled and done with. That's our little personal bargain in the matter of the lamentable accident with the chair. We are now talking of bigger business—not hundreds, but thousands, and not one of them, but a lot. Come now, a mind like yours should be wide enough to admit of a broad and large view of things. If I refrain from exposing this charming scheme of yours I shall be promoting a piece of scandalous robbery. Very well then, I want my promotion money, in the regular way. Can I shut my eyes and allow a piece of iniquity like this to go on unchecked, without getting anything by way of damages for myself? Perish the thought! When all expenses are paid, and the confederates are sent off with as little as they will take, you and I will divide fairly, Mr. Mallows, respectable brothers in rascality. Mind, I might say we'd divide to begin with, and leave you to pay expenses, but I am always fair to a partner in anything of this sort. I shall just want a little guarantee, you know—it's safest in such matters as these; say a bill at six months for ten thousand pounds—which is very low. When a satisfactory division is made you shall have the bill back. Come—I have a bill-stamp ready, being so much convinced of your reasonableness as to buy it this morning, though it cost five pounds."

"But that's nonsense—you're trying to impose. I'll give you anything reasonable—half is out of the question. What, after all the trouble and worry and risk that I've had—"

"Which would suffice for no more than to put you in gaol if I held up my finger!"

"But hang it, be reasonable! You're a mighty clever man, and you've got me on the hip, as I admit. Say ten per cent."

"You're wasting time, and presently the men will be back. Your choice is between making half, or making none, and going to gaol into the bargain. Choose!"

"But just consider—"

"Choose!"

Mallows looked despairingly about him. "But really," he said, "I want the money more than you think. I—"

"For the last time—choose!"

Mallows's despairing gaze stopped at the enamelling oven. "Well, well," he said, "if I must, I must, I suppose. But I warn you, you may regret it."

"Oh dear no, I'm not so pessimistic. Come, you wrote a cheque—now I'll write the bill. 'Six months after date, pay to me or my order the sum of ten thousand pounds for value received'—excellent value too, *I* think. There you are!"

When the bill was written and signed, Mallows scribbled his acceptance with more readiness than might have been expected. Then he rose, and said with something of brisk cheerfulness in his tone, "Well, that's done, and the least said the soonest mended. You've won it, and I won't grumble any more. I think I've done this thing pretty neatly, eh? Come and see the 'works.'"

Every other part of the place was empty of machinery. There were a good many finished frames and wheels, bought separately, and now in course of being fitted together for sale; and there were many more complete bicycles of cheap but showy make to which nothing needed to be done but to fix the red and gold "transfer" of the "Avalanche" company. Then Mallows opened the tall iron door of the enamelling oven.

"See this," he said; "this is the enamelling oven. Get in and look round. The frames and other different parts hang on the racks after the enamel is laid on, and all those gas jets are lighted to harden it by heat. Do you see that deeper part there by the back?—go closer."

Dorrington felt a push at his back and the door was swung to with a bang, and the latch dropped. He was in the dark, trapped in a great iron chamber. "I warned you," shouted Mallows from without; "I warned you you might regret it!" And instantly Dorrington's nostrils were filled with the smell of escaping gas. He realised his peril on the instant. Mallows had given him the bill with the idea of silencing him by murder and recovering it. He had pushed him into the oven and had turned on the gas. It was dark, but to light a match would mean death instantly, and without the match it must be death by suffocation and poison of gas in a very few minutes. To appeal to Mallows was useless—Dorrington knew too much. It would seem that at last a horribly-fitting retribution had overtaken Dorrington in death by a mode parallel to that which he and his creatures had prepared for others. Dorrington's victims had drowned in water—or at least Crofton's had, for I never ascertained definitely whether anybody had met his death by the tank after the Croftons had taken service with Dorrington—and now Dorrington himself was to drown in gas. The oven was of sheet iron, fastened by a latch in the centre. Dorrington flung himself desperately against the door, and it gave outwardly at the extreme bottom. He snatched a loose angle-iron with which his hand came in contact, dashed against the door once more, and thrust the iron through where it strained open. Then, with another tremendous plunge, he drove the door a little more outward and raised the angle-iron in the crack; then once more, and raised it again. He was near to losing his senses, when, with one more plunge, the catch of the latch, not designed for such treatment, suddenly gave way, the door flew open, and Dorrington, blue in the face, staring, stumbling and gasping, came staggering out into the fresher air, followed by a gush of gas.

Mallows had retreated to the rooms behind, and thither Dorrington followed him, gaining vigour and fury at every step. At sight of him the wretched Mallows sank in a corner, sighing and shivering with terror. Dorrington reached him and clutched him by the collar. There should be no more honour between these two thieves now. He would drag Mallows forth and proclaim him aloud; and he would keep that £10,000 bill. He hauled the struggling wretch across the room, tearing off the crêpe whiskers as he came, while Mallows supplicated and whined, fearing that it might be the other's design to imprison *him* in the enamelling oven. But at the door of the room against that containing the oven their progress came to an end, for the escaped gas had reached the lighted candle, and with one loud report the partition wall fell in, half burying Mallows where he lay, and knocking Dorrington over.

Windows fell out of the building, and men broke through the front gate, climbed into the ruined rooms and stopped the still escaping gas. When the two men and the boy returned, with the conspirator who had been in charge of the works, they found a crowd from the hardware and cycle factories thereabout, surveying with great interest the spectacle of the extrication of Mr. Paul Mallows, managing director of the "Indestructible Bicycle Company," from the broken bricks, mortar, bicycles and transfers of the "Avalanche Bicycle and Tyre Company, Limited," and the preparations for carrying him to a surgeon's where his broken leg might be set. As for Dorrington, a crushed hat and a torn coat were all his hurts, beyond a few scratches. And in a couple of hours it was all over Birmingham, and spreading to other places, that the business of the "Avalanche Bicycle and Tyre Company" consisted of sticking brilliant labels on factors' bicycles, bought in batches; for the whole thing was thrown open to the general gaze by the explosion. So that when, next day, Lant won the fifty miles race in London, he was greeted with ironical shouts of "Gum on yer transfer!" "Hi! mind yer label!" "Where did you steal that bicycle?" "Sold yer shares?" and so forth.

Somehow the "Avalanche Bicycle and Tyre Company, Limited," never went to allotment. It was said that a few people in remote and benighted spots, where news never came till it was in the history books, had applied for shares, but the bankers returned their money, doubtless to their extreme disappointment. It was found politic, also, that Mr. Paul Mallows should retire from the directorate of the "Indestructible Bicycle Company"—a concern which is still, I believe, flourishing exceedingly.

As for Dorrington, he had his hundred pounds reward. But the bill for £10,000 he never presented. Why, I do not altogether know, unless he found that Mr. Mallows's financial position, as he had hinted, was not altogether so good as was supposed. At any rate, it was found among the notes and telegrams in this case in the Dorrington deed-box.

The Case of Mr. Loftus Deacon

I

THIS WAS A CASE THAT helped to give Dorrington much of that reputation which unfortunately too often enabled him to profit himself far beyond the extent to which his clients intended. It occurred some few years back, and there was such a stir at the time over the mysterious death of Mr. Loftus Deacon that it well paid Dorrington to use his utmost diligence in an honest effort to uncover the mystery. It gave him one of his best advertisements, though indeed it occasioned him less trouble in the unravelling than many a less interesting case. There were scarcely any memoranda of the affair among Dorrington's papers, beyond entries of fees paid, and I have almost entirely relied upon the account given me by Mr. Stone, manager in the employ of the firm owning the premises in which Mr. Deacon died.

These premises consisted of a large building let out in expensive flats, one of the first places built with that design in the West-End of London. The building was one of three, all belonging to the firm I have mentioned, and numbered 1, 2 and 3, Bedford Mansions. They stood in the St. James's district, and Mr. Loftus Deacon's quarters were in No. 2.

Mr. Deacon's magnificent collection of oriental porcelain will be remembered as long as any in the national depositories; much of it was for a long while lent, and, by Mr. Deacon's will, passed permanently into possession of the nation. His collection of oriental arms, however, was broken up and sold, as were also his other innumerable objects of Eastern art—lacquers, carvings, and so forth. He was a wealthy man, this Mr. Deacon, a bachelor of sixty, and his whole life was given to his collections. He was currently reported to spend some £15,000 a year on them, and, in addition, would make inroads into capital for special purchases at the great sales. People wondered where all the things were kept. And indeed they had reason, for Mr. Deacon's personal establishment was but a suite of rooms on the ground floor of Bedford Mansions. But the bulk of the collections were housed at various museums—indeed it was a matter of banter among his acquaintances that Mr. Loftus Deacon made the taxpayers warehouse most of his things; moreover, the flat was a large one—it occupied almost the whole of the ground-floor of the building, and it overflowed with the choicest of its tenant's possessions. There were eight large and lofty rooms, as well as the lobby, scullery and so forth, and every one was full. The walls were hung with the most precious *kakemono* and *nishikiyé* of Japan; and glass cabinets stood everywhere, packed with porcelain and faience—celadon, peach-bloom, and blue and white, Satsuma, Raku, Ninsei, and Arita—many a small piece worth its weight in gold over and over and over again. At places on the wall, among the *kakemono* and pictures of the *ukioyé*, were trophies of arms. Two suits of ancient Japanese armour, each complete and each the production of one of the most eminent of the Miochin family, were exhibited on stands, and swords stood in many corners and lay in many racks. Innumerable drawers contained specimens of the greatest lacquer ware of Korin, Shunsho, Kajikawa, Koyetsu, and Ritsuo, each in its wadded brocade *fukusa* with the light wooden box encasing all. In more glass cabinets stood *netsuké* and *okimono* of ivory, bronze, wood, and lacquer. There were a few gods and goddesses, and conspicuous among them two life-sized gilt Buddhas beamed mildly over all from the shelves on which they were raised. By the operation of natural selection it came about that the choicest of all Mr. Deacon's possessions were collected in these rooms. Here were none of the great cumbersome pots, good in their way, but made of old time merely for the European market. Of all that was Japanese every piece was the best and rarest, consequently, in almost every case, of small dimensions, as is the way of the greatest of the wares of old Japan. And of all the precious contents of these rooms everything was oriental in its origin except the contents of one case, which displayed specimens of the most magnificent goldsmiths' and silver-smiths' work of mediæval Europe. It stood in the room which Mr. Loftus Deacon used as his sitting-room, and more than one of his visitors had wondered that such valuable property was not kept at a banker's. This view, however, always surprised and irritated Mr. Deacon. "Keep it at a banker's?" he would say. "Why not melt it down at once? The things are works of art, things of beauty, and that's why I have them, not merely because they're gold and silver. To shut them up in a strong-room would be the next thing to destroying them altogether. Why not lock the whole of my collections in safes, and never look at them? They are all valuable. But if they are not to be seen I would rather have the money they cost." So the gold and silver stood in its case, to the blinking wonderment of messengers and porters whose errands took them into Mr. Loftus Deacon's sitting-room. The contents of this case were the only occasion, however, of Mr. Deacon's straying from oriental paths in building up his collection. There they stood, but he made no attempt to add to them. He went about his daily hunting, bargaining, cataloguing, cleaning, and exhibiting to friends, but all his new treasures were from the East, and most were Japanese. His chief visitors were travelling buyers of curiosities; little Japanese who had come to England to study medicine and were paying their terms by the sale of heirlooms in pottery and lacquer; porters from Christie's and Foster's; and sometimes men from Copleston's—the odd emporium by the riverside where lions and monkeys, porcelain and savage weapons were bought and sold close by the ships that brought them home. The travellers were suspicious and cunning; the Japanese were bright, polite, and dignified, and the men from Copleston's were wiry, hairy and amphibious; one was an enormously muscular little hunchback nicknamed Slackjaw—a quaint and rather repulsive compound of showman, sailor and half-caste rough; and all were like mermen, more or less. These curious people came and went, and Mr. Deacon went on buying, cataloguing, and joying in his possessions. It was the happiest possible life for a lonely old man with his tastes and his means of gratifying them, and it went placidly on till one Wednesday mid-day. Then Mr. Deacon was found dead in his rooms in most extraordinary and, it seemed, altogether unaccountable circumstances.

There was but one door leading into Mr. Deacon's rooms from the open corridor of the building, and this was immediately opposite the large street door. When one entered from the street one ascended three or four broad marble steps, pushed open one of a pair of glazed swing doors and found oneself facing the door by which Mr. Deacon entered and left his quarters. There had originally been other doors into the corridor from some of the rooms, but those Mr. Deacon had had blocked up, so making the flat entirely self-contained. Just by the glazed swing doors which I have spoken of, and in full view of the old gentleman's door, the hall-porter's box stood. It was glazed on all sides, and the porter sat so that Mr. Deacon's door was always before his eyes, and, so long as he was there, it was very unlikely that anybody or anything could leave or enter by that door unobserved by him. It is important to remember this, in view of what happened on the occasion

I am writing of. There was one other exterior door to Mr. Deacon's flat, and one only. It gave upon the back spiral staircase, and was usually kept locked. This staircase had no outlet to the corridors, but merely extended from the housekeeper's rooms at the top of the building to the basement. It was little used, and then only by servants, for it gave access only to the rooms on its own side. There was no way from this staircase to the outer street except through the private rooms of the tenants, or through those of the housekeeper.

That Wednesday morning things had happened precisely in the ordinary way. Mr. Deacon had risen and breakfasted as usual. He was alone, with his newspaper and his morning letters, when his breakfast was taken in and when it was removed. He had remained in his rooms till between twelve and one o'clock. Goods had arrived for him (this was an almost daily occurrence), and one or two ordinary visitors had called and gone away again. It was Mr. Deacon's habit to lunch at his club, and at about a quarter to one, or thereabout, he had come out, locked his door, and leaving his usual message that he should be at the club for an hour or two, in case anybody called, he had left the building. At about one, however, he had returned hurriedly, having forgotten some letters. "I didn't give you any letters for the post, did I, Beard, before I went out?" he asked the porter. And the porter replied that he had not. Mr. Deacon thereupon crossed the corridor, entered his door, and shut it behind him.

He had been gone but a few seconds, when there arose an outcry from within the rooms—a shout followed in a breath by a loud cry of pain, and then silence. Beard, the porter, ran to the door and knocked, but there was no reply. "Did you call, sir?" he shouted, and knocked again, but still without response. The door was shut, and it had a latch lock with no exterior handle. Beard, who had had an uncle die of apoplexy, was now thoroughly alarmed, and shouted up the speaking tube for the housekeeper's keys. In course of a few minutes they were brought, and Beard and the housekeeper entered.

The lobby was as usual, and the sitting-room was in perfect order. But in the room beyond Mr. Loftus Deacon lay in a pool of blood, with two large and fearful gashes in his head. Not a soul was in any of the rooms, though the two men, first shutting the outer door, searched diligently. All windows and doors were shut, and the rooms were tenantless and undisturbed, except that on the floor lay Mr. Deacon in his blood at the foot of a pedestal whereupon there squatted, with serenely fierce grin, the god Hachiman, gilt and painted, carrying in one of his four hands a snake, in another a mace, in a third a small human figure, and in the fourth a heavy, straight, guardless sword; and all around furniture, cabinets, porcelain, lacquer and everything else lay undisturbed.

At first sight of the tragedy the porter had sent the lift-man for the police, and soon they arrived, and a surgeon with them. For the surgeon there was very little to do. Mr. Deacon was dead. Either of the two frightful gashes in the head would have been fatal, and they had obviously both been delivered with the same instrument—something heavy and exceedingly sharp.

The police now set themselves to close investigation. The porter was certain that nobody had entered the rooms that morning who had not afterwards left. He was sure that nobody had entered unobserved, and he was sure that Mr. Deacon had re-entered his chambers unaccompanied. Working, therefore, on the assumption that the murderer could not have entered by the front door, the police turned their attention to the back door and the windows. The door to the back staircase was locked, and the key was in the lock and inside. Therefore they considered the windows. There were but three of these that looked upon the street, two in one room and one in another, but these were shut and fastened within. Other rooms were lighted by windows looking upon lighting-wells, some being supplied with reflectors. All these windows were found to be quite undisturbed, and fastened within, except one. This window was in the bedroom, and, though it was shut, the catch was not fastened. The porter declared that it was Mr. Deacon's practice invariably to fasten every shut window, a thing he was always very careful about. Moreover, the window now found unfastened and shut was always left open a foot or so all day, to air the bedroom. More, a housemaid was brought who had that morning made the bed and dusted the room. The window was opened, she said, when she had entered the room, and she had left it so, as she always did. Therefore, shut as it was, but not fastened, it seemed plain that this window must have given exit to the murderer, since no other way appeared possible. Also, to shut the window behind him would be the fugitive's natural policy. The lower panes were of ground glass, and at least pursuit would be delayed.

The window looked upon a lighting-well, and the concreted floor of the basement was but fifteen or twenty feet below. Careful inquiries disclosed the fact that a man had been at work painting the joinery about this well-bottom. He was a man of very indifferent character—had in fact "done time"—and he was employed for odd jobs by way of charity, being some sort of connection of a member of the firm owning the buildings. He had, indeed, received a good education, fitted to place him in a very different position from that in which he now found himself, but he was a black sheep. He drank, he gambled, and finally he stole. His relatives helped him again and again, but their efforts were useless, and now he was indebted to one of them for his present occupation at a pound a week. The police, of course, knew something of him, and postponed questioning him directly until they had investigated a little further. It might be that Mr. Deacon's death was the work of a conspiracy wherein more than one had participated.

II

The next morning (Thursday) Mr. Henry Colson was an early caller at Dorrington's office. Mr. Colson was a thin, grizzled man of sixty or thereabout, who had been a close friend—the only intimate friend, indeed—of Mr. Loftus Deacon. He was a widower, and he lived in rooms scarce two hundred yards distant from Bedford Mansions, where his friend had died.

"My business, Mr. Dorrington," he said, "is in connection with the terrible death of my old friend Mr. Loftus Deacon, of which you no doubt have heard or read in the morning papers."

"Yes," Dorrington assented, "both in this morning's papers and the evening papers of yesterday."

"Very good. I may tell you that I am sole executor under Mr. Deacon's will. The will indeed is in my possession (I am a retired solicitor), and there happens to be a sum set apart in that will out of which I am to defray any expenses that may arise in connection with his death. It really seems to me that I should be quite justified in using some part of that sum in paying for inquiries to be conducted by such an experienced man as yourself, into the cause of my poor friend's death. At any rate, I wish you to make such inquiries, even if I have to pay the fees myself. I am convinced that there is something very extraordinary—something very deep—in the tragedy. The police are pottering about, of course, and keeping very mysterious as to the matter, but I expect that's simply because they know nothing. They have made no arrest, and perhaps every minute of delay is making the thing more difficult. As executor, of course, I have access to the rooms. Can you come and look at them now?"

"Oh yes," Dorrington answered, reaching for his hat. "I suppose there's no doubt of the case being one of murder? Suicide is not likely, I take it?"

"Oh no—certainly not. He was scarcely the sort of man to commit suicide, I should say. And he was as cheerful as he could be the afternoon before, when I last saw him. Besides, the surgeon says it's nothing of the kind. A man committing suicide doesn't gash himself twice over the head, or even once. And in this case the first blow would have made him incapable of another."

"I have heard nothing about the weapon," Dorrington remarked, as they entered a cab. "Has it been found?"

"That's a difficulty," Mr. Colson answered. "It would seem not. Of course there are numbers of weapons about the place—Japanese swords and what not—any one of which *might* have caused such injuries. But there are no bloodstains on any of them."

"Is any article of value missing?"

"I believe not. Everything seemed to be in its place, so far as I noticed yesterday. But then I was not there long, and was too much agitated to notice very particularly. At any rate the old gold and silver plate had not been disturbed. He kept that in a large case in his sitting-room, and it would certainly be the plate that the murderer would have made for first, if robbery had been his object."

Mr. Colson gave Dorrington the other details of the case, already set forth in this account, and presently the cab stopped before No. 2, Bedford Mansions. The body, of course, had been removed, but otherwise the rooms had not been disturbed. The porter let them into the chambers by aid of the housekeeper's key.

"They don't seem to have found his keys," Mr. Colson explained, "and that will be troublesome for me, I expect, presently. He usually carried them with him, but they were not on the body when found."

"That may be important," Dorrington said. "But let us look at the rooms."

They walked through the large apartments one after the other, and Dorrington glanced casually about him as he went. Presently Mr. Colson stopped, struck with an idea. "Ah!" he said, more to himself than to Dorrington. "I will just see."

He turned quickly back into the room they had just quitted, and made for the broad shelf that ran the length of the wall at about the height of an ordinary table. "Yes!" he cried. "It is! It's gone!"

"What is gone?"

"The sword—the Masamuné!"

The whole surface of the shelf, covered with a silk cloth, was occupied by Japanese swords and dirks with rich mountings. Most lay on their sides in rows, but two or three were placed in the lacquered racks. Mr. Colson stood and pointed at a rack which was standing alone and swordless. "That is where it was," he said. "I saw it—was talking about it, in fact—the afternoon before. No, it's nowhere about. It's not like any of the others. Let me see." And Mr. Colson, much excited, hurried from room to room wherever swords were kept, searching for the missing specimen.

"No," he said at last, looking strangely startled; "It's gone. And I think we are near the soul of the mystery." He spoke in hushed, uneasy tones, and his eyes gave token of strange apprehension.

"What is it?" Dorrington asked. "What about this sword?"

"Come into the sitting-room." Mr. Colson led Dorrington away from the scene of Mr. Deacon's end, away from the empty sword rack and from under the shadow of the grinning god with its four arms, its snake, and its threatening sword. "I don't think I'm very superstitious," Mr. Colson proceeded, "but I really feel that I can talk more freely about the matter in here."

They sat at the table, over against the case of plate, and Mr. Colson went on. "The sword I speak of," he said, "was much prized by my poor friend, who brought it with him from Japan nearly twenty years back—not many years after the civil war there, in fact. It was a very ancient specimen—of the fourteenth century, I think—and the work of the famous swordsmith Masamuné. Masamuné's work is very rarely met with, it seems, and Mr. Deacon felt himself especially fortunate in securing this example. It is the only piece of Masamuné's work in the collection. I may tell you that a sword by one of the great old masters is one of the rarest of all the rarities that come from Japan. The possessors of the best keep them rather than sell them at any price. Such swords were handed down from father to son for many generations, and a Japanese of the old school would have been disgraced had he parted with his father's blade even under the most pressing necessity. The mounts he might possibly sell, if he were in very bad circumstances, but the blade never. Of course, such a thing *has* occurred—and it occurred in this very case, as you shall hear. But as an almost invariable rule the Japanese *samurai* would part with his life by starvation rather than with his father's sword by sale. Such swords would never be stolen, either, for there was a firm belief that a faithful spirit resided in each, which would bring terrible disaster on any wrongful possessor. Each sword had its own name, just as the legendary sword of King Arthur had, and a man's social standing was judged, not by his house nor by his dress, but by the two swords in his girdle. The ancient sword-smiths wore court dress and made votive offerings when they forged their best blades, and the gods were supposed to assist and to watch over the career of the weapon. Thus you will understand that such an article was apt to become an object almost of worship among the *samurai* or warrior-class in Old Japan. And now to come to the sword in question. It was a long sword or *katana* (the swords, as you know, were worn in pairs, and the smaller was called the *wakizashi*), and it was mounted very handsomely with fittings by a great metal worker of the Goto family. The signature of the great Masamuné himself was engraved in the usual place—on the iron tang within the hilt. Mr. Deacon bought the weapon of its possessor, a man of some distinction before the overthrow of the Shogun in 1868, but who was reduced to deep poverty by the change in affairs. Mr. Deacon came across him in his direst straits, when his children were near to starvation, and the man sold the sword for a sum that was a little fortune to him, though it only represented some four or five pounds of our money. Mr. Deacon was always very proud of his treasure—indeed it was said to be the only blade by Masamuné in Europe; and the two Japanese things that he had always most longed for, I have heard him say, were a Masamuné sword and a piece of violet lacquer—that precious lacquer the secret of making which died long ago. The Masamuné he acquired, as I have been telling you, but the violet lacquer he never once encountered.

"Six months or so back, Deacon received a visit from a Japanese— taller than usual for a Japanese (I have seen him myself) and with the refined type of face characteristic of some of the higher class of his country. His name was Keigo Kanamaro, his card said, and he introduced himself as the son of Keigo Kiyotaki, the man who had sold Deacon his sword. He had come to England and had found my friend after much inquiry, he said, expressly to take back his father's *katana*. His father was dead, and he desired to place the sword in his tomb, that the soul of the old man might rest in peace, undisturbed by the disgrace that had fallen upon him by the sale of the sword that had been his and his ancestors' for hundreds of years back. The father had vowed when he had received the sword in his turn from Kanamaro's grandfather, never to part with it, but had broken his vow under pressure of want. He (the son) had earned money as a merchant (an immeasurable descent for a *samurai* with the feelings of the old school), and he was prepared to buy back the Masamuné blade with the Goto mountings for a much higher price than his father had received for it."

"And I suppose Deacon wouldn't sell it?" Dorrington asked.

"No," Mr. Colson replied. "He wouldn't have sold it at any price, I'm sure. Well, Kanamaro pressed him very urgently, and called again and again. He was very gentlemanly and very dignified, but he was very earnest. He apologised for making a commercial offer, assured Deacon that he was quite aware that he was no mere buyer and seller, but pleaded the urgency of his case. 'It is not here as in Japan,' he said, 'among us, the *samurai* of the old days. You have your beliefs, we have ours. It is my religion that I must place the *katana* in my father's grave. My father disgraced himself and sold his sword in order that I might not starve when I was a little child. I would rather that he had let me die, but since I am alive, and I know that you have the sword, I must take it and lay it by his bones. I will make an offer. Instead of giving you money, I will give you another sword—a sword worth as much money as my father's—perhaps more. I have had it sent from Japan since I first saw you. It is a blade made by the great Yukiyasu, and it has a scabbard and mountings by an older and greater master than the Goto who made those for my father's sword.' But it happened that Deacon already had two swords by Yukiyasu, while of Masamuné he had only the one. So he tried to reason the Japanese out of his fancy. But that was useless. Kanamaro called again and again and got to be quite a nuisance. He left off for a month or two, but about a fortnight ago he appeared again. He grew angry and forgot his oriental politeness. 'The English have the English ways,' he said, 'and we have ours—yes, though many of my foolish countrymen are in haste to be the same as the English are. We have our beliefs, and we have our knowledge, and I tell you that there are things which you would call superstition, but which are very real! Our old gods are not all dead yet, I tell you! In the old times no man would wear or keep another man's sword. Why? Because the great sword has a soul just as a man has, and it knows and the gods know! No man kept another's sword who did not fall into terrible misfortune and death, sooner or later. Give me my father's *katana* and save yourself. My father weeps in my ears at night, and I must bring him his *katana!*' I was talking to poor Deacon, as I told you, only on Tuesday afternoon, and he told me that Kanamaro had been there again the day before, in a frantic state—so bad, indeed, that Deacon thought of applying to the Japanese legation to have him taken care of, for he seemed quite mad. 'Mind, you foolish man!' he said. 'My gods still live, and they are strong! My father wanders on the dark path and cannot go to his gods without the swords in his girdle. His father asks of his vow! Between here and Japan there is a great sea, but my father may walk even here, looking for his *katana*, and he is angry! I go away for a little. But my gods know, and my father knows!' And then he took himself off. And now"—Mr. Colson nodded towards the next room and dropped his voice—"now poor Deacon is dead and the sword is gone!"

"Kanamaro has not been seen about the place, I suppose, since the visit you speak of, on Monday?" Dorrington asked.

"No. And I particularly asked as to yesterday morning. The hall-porter swears that no Japanese came to the place."

"As to the letters, now. You say that when Mr. Deacon came back, after having left, apparently to get his lunch, he said he came for forgotten letters. Were any such letters afterwards found?"

"Yes—there were three, lying on this very table, stamped ready for postage."

"Where are they now?"

"I have them at my chambers. I opened them in the presence of the police in charge of the case. There was nothing very important about them—appointments and so forth, merely—and so the police left them in my charge, as executor."

"Nevertheless I should like to see them. Not just now, but presently. I think I must see this man presently—the man who was painting in the basement below the window that is supposed to have been shut by the murderer in his escape. That is if the police haven't frightened him."

"Very well, we'll see after him as soon as you like. There was just one other thing—rather a curious coincidence, though of course there can't be anything in such a superstitious fancy—but I think I told you that Deacon's body was found lying at the feet of the four-handed god in the other room?"

"Yes."

"Just so." Mr. Colson seemed to think a little more of the superstitious fancy than he confessed. "Just so," he said again. "At the feet of the god, and immediately under the hand carrying the sword; it is not wooden, but an actual steel sword, in fact."

"I noticed that."

"Yes. Now that is a figure of Hachiman, the Japanese god of war—a recent addition to the collection and a very ancient specimen. Deacon bought it at Copleston's only a few days ago—indeed it arrived here on Wednesday morning. Deacon was telling me about it on Tuesday afternoon. He bought it because of its extraordinary design, showing such signs of Indian influence. Hachiman is usually represented with no more than the usual number of a man's arms, and with no weapon but a sword. This is the only image of Hachiman that Deacon ever saw or heard of with four arms. And after he had bought it he ascertained that this was said to be one of the idols that carry with them ill-luck from the moment they leave their temples. One of Copleston's men confided to Deacon that the lascar seamen and stokers on board the ship that brought it over swore that everything went wrong from the moment that Hachiman came on board—and indeed the vessel was nearly lost off Finisterre. And Copleston himself, the man said, was glad to be quit of it. Things had disappeared in the most extraordinary and unaccountable manner, and other things had been found smashed (notably a large porcelain vase) without any human agency, after standing near the figure. Well," Mr. Colson concluded, "after all that, and remembering what Kanamaro said about the gods of his country who watch over ancient swords, it *does* seem odd, doesn't it, that as soon as poor Deacon gets the thing he should be found stricken dead at its feet?"

Dorrington was thinking. "Yes," he said presently, "it is certainly a strange affair altogether. Let us see the odd-job man now—the man who was in the basement below the window. Or rather, find out where he is and leave me to find him."

Mr. Colson stepped out and spoke with the hall-porter. Presently he returned with news. "He's gone!" he said. "Bolted!"

"What—the man who was in the basement?"

"Yes. It seems the police questioned him pretty closely yesterday, and he seized the first opportunity to cut and run."

"Do you know what they asked him?"

"Examined him generally, I suppose, as to what he had observed at the time. The only thing he seems to have said was that he heard a window shut at about one o'clock. Questioned further, he got into confusion and equivocation, more especially when they mentioned a ladder which is kept in a passage close by where he was painting. It seems they had examined this before speaking to him, and found it had been just recently removed and put back. It was thick with dust, except just where it had been taken hold of to shift, and there the hand-marks were quite clean. Nobody was in the basement but Dowden (that is the man's name), and nobody else could have shifted that ladder without his hearing and knowing of it. Moreover, the ladder was just the length to reach Deacon's window. They asked if he had seen anybody move the ladder, and he most anxiously and vehemently declared that he had not. A little while after he was missing, and he hasn't reappeared."

"And they let him go!" Dorrington exclaimed. "What fools!"

"He *may* know something about it, of course," Colson said dubiously; "but with that sword missing, and knowing what we do of Kanamaro's anxiety to get it at any cost, and—and"—he glanced toward the other room where the idol stood—"and one thing and another, it seems to me we should look in another direction."

"We will look in all directions," Dorrington replied. "Kanamaro may have enlisted Dowden's help. Do you know where to find Kanamaro?"

"Yes. Deacon has had letters from him, which I have seen. He lived in lodgings near the British Museum."

"Very well. Now, do you happen to know whether a night porter is kept at this place?"

"No, there is none. The outer door is shut at twelve. Anybody coming home after that must ring up the housekeeper by the electric bell."

"The tenants do not have keys for the outer door?"

"No; none but keys for their own rooms."

"Good. Now, Mr. Colson, I want to think things over a little. Would you care to go at once and ascertain whether or not Kanamaro is still at the address you speak of?"

"Certainly, I will. Perhaps I should have told you that, though he knows me slightly, he has never spoken of his father's sword to me, and does not know that I know anything about it. He seems, indeed, to have spoken about it to nobody but Deacon himself. He was very proud and reticent in the matter; and now that Deacon is dead, he probably thinks nobody alive knows of the matter of the sword but himself. If he is at home what shall I do?"

"In that case keep him in sight and communicate with me, or with the police. I shall stay here for a little while. Then I shall get the hall-porter (if you will instruct him before you go) to show me the ladder and the vicinity of Dowden's operations. Also, I think I shall look at the back staircase."

"But that was found locked, with the key inside."

"Well, well, there *are* ways of managing that, as you would know if you knew as much about housebreaking as I do. But we'll see."

III

Mr. Colson took a cab for Kanamaro's lodgings. Kanamaro was not in, he found, and he had given notice to leave his rooms. The servant at the door thought that he was going abroad, since his boxes were being packed, apparently for that purpose. The servant did not know at what time he would be back.

Mr. Colson thought for a moment of reporting these facts at once to Dorrington, but on second thoughts he determined to hurry to the City and make inquiry at some of the shipping offices as to the vessels soon to leave for Japan. On the way, however, he bethought him to buy a shipping paper and gather his information from that. He found what he wanted from the paper, but he kept the cab on its way, for he happened to know a man in authority at the Anglo-Malay Company's office, and it might be a good thing to take a look at their passenger list. Their next ship for Yokohama was to sail in a few days.

But he found it unnecessary to see the passenger list. As he entered one of the row of swing doors which gave access to the large general and inquiry office of the steamship company, he perceived Keigo Kanamaro leaving by another. Kanamaro had not seen him. Mr. Colson hesitated for a moment, and then turned and followed him.

And now Mr. Colson became suddenly seized with a burning fancy to play the subtle detective on his own account. Plainly Kanamaro feared nothing, walking about thus openly, and taking his passage for Japan at the chief office of the first line of steamships that anybody would think of who contemplated a voyage to Japan, instead of leaving the country, as he might have done, by some indirect route, and shipping for Japan from a foreign port. Doubtless, he still supposed that nobody knew of his errand in search of his father's sword. Mr. Colson quickened his pace and came up beside the Japanese.

Kanamaro was a well-made man of some five feet eight or nine—remarkably tall for a native of Dai Nippon. His cheek-bones had not the prominence noticeable in the Japanese of the lower classes, and his pale oval face and aquiline nose gave token of high *sikozu* family. His hair only was of the coarse black that is seen on the heads of all Japanese. He perceived Mr. Colson, and stopped at once with a grave bow.

"Good morning," Mr. Colson said. "I saw you leaving the steamship office, and wondered whether or not you were going to leave us."

"Yes—I go home to Japan by the next departing ship," Kanamaro answered. He spoke with an excellent pronunciation, but with the intonation and the suppression of short syllables peculiar to his countrymen who speak English. "My beesness is finished."

Mr. Colson's suspicions were more than strengthened—almost confirmed. He commanded his features, however, and replied, as he walked by Keigo's side, "Ah! your visit has been successful, then?"

"It has been successful," Kanamaro answered, "at a very great cost."

"At a very great cost?"

"Yes—I did not expect to have to do what I have done—I should once not have believed it possible that I *could* do it. But"—Kanamaro checked himself hastily and resumed his grave reserve—"but that is private beesness, and not for me to disturb you with."

Mr. Colson had the tact to leave that line of fishing alone for a little. He walked a few yards in silence, and then asked, with his eyes furtively fixed on the face of the Japanese, "Do you know of the god Hachiman?"

"It is Hachiman the warrior; him of eight flags," Kanamaro replied. "Yes, I know, of course."

He spoke as though he would banish the subject. But Mr. Colson went on—

"Did he preside over the forging of ancient sword-blades in Japan?" he asked.

"I do not know of preside—that is a new word. But the great workers of the steel, those who made the *katana* in the times of Yoshitsuné and Taiko-Sama, they hung curtains and made offerings to Hachiman when they forged a blade—yes. The great Muramasa and the great Masamuné and Sanénori—they forged their blades at the foot of Hachiman. And it is believed that the god Inari came unseen with his hammer and forged the steel too. Though Hachiman is Buddhist and Inari is Shinto. But these are not things to talk about. There is one religion, which is yours, and there is another religion, which is mine, and it is not good that we talk together of them. There are things that people call superstition when they are of another religion, though they may be very true."

They walked a little farther, and then Mr. Colson, determined to penetrate Kanamaro's mask of indifference, observed—

"It's a very sad thing this about Mr. Deacon."

"What is that?" asked Kanamaro, stolidly.

"Why, it is in all the newspapers!"

"The newspapers I do not read at all."

"Mr. Deacon has been killed—murdered in his rooms! He was found lying dead at the feet of Hachiman the god."

"Indeed!" Kanamaro answered politely, but with something rather like stolid indifference. "That is very sad. I am sorry. I did not know he had a Hachiman."

"And they say," Mr. Colson pursued, "that *something* has been taken!"

"Ah, yes," Kanamaro answered, just as coolly; "there were many things of much value in the rooms." And after a little while he added, "I see it is a little late. You will excuse me, for I must go to lunch at my lodgings. Good-day."

He bowed, shook hands, and hailed a cab. Mr. Colson heard him direct the cabman to his lodgings, and then, in another cab, Mr. Colson made for Dorrington's office.

Kanamaro's stolidity, the lack of anything like surprise at the news of Mr. Deacon's death, his admission that he had finished his business in England successfully—these things placed the matter beyond all doubt in Mr. Colson's mind. Plainly he felt so confident that none knew of his errand in England, that he took things with perfect coolness, and even ventured so far as to speak of the murder in very near terms—to say that he did not expect to have to do what he had done, and would not have believed it possible that he *could* do it—though, to be sure, he checked himself at once before going farther. Certainly Dorrington must be told at once. That would be better than going to the police, perhaps, for possibly the police might not consider the evidence sufficient to justify an arrest, and Dorrington may have ascertained something in the meantime.

Dorrington had not been heard of at his office since leaving there early in the morning. So Mr. Colson saw Hicks, and arranged that a man should be put on to watch Kanamaro, and should be sent instantly, before he could leave his lodgings again. Then Mr. Colson hurried to Bedford Mansions.

There he saw the housekeeper. From him he learned that Dorrington had left some time since, promising either to be back or to telegraph during the afternoon. Also, he learned that Beard, the hall-porter, was in a great state of indignation and anxiety as a consequence of the discovery that he was being watched by the police. He had got a couple of days leave of absence to go and see his mother, who was ill, and he found his intentions and destination a matter of pressing inquiry. Mr. Colson assured the housekeeper that he might promise Beard a speedy respite from the attentions of the police, and went to his lunch.

IV

AFTER HIS LUNCH MR. COLSON CALLED and called again at Bedford Mansions, but neither Dorrington nor his telegram had been heard of. At something near five o'clock, however, when he had made up his mind to wait, restless as he was, Dorrington appeared, fresh and complacent.

"Hope you haven't been waiting long?" he asked. "Fact is I got no opportunity for lunch till after four, so I had it then. I think I'd fairly earned it. The case is finished."

"Finished? But there's Kanamaro to be arrested. I've found—"

"No, no—I don't think anybody will be arrested at all; you'll read about it in the evening papers in an hour, I expect. But come into the rooms. I have some things to show you."

"But I assure you," Mr. Colson said, as he entered the door of Deacon's rooms, "I assure you that I got as good as a confession from Kanamaro—he let it slip in ignorance of what I knew. Why do you say that nobody is to be arrested?"

"Because there's nobody alive who is responsible for Mr. Deacon's death. But come—let me show you the whole thing; it's very simple."

He led the way to the room where the body had been found, and paused before the four-armed idol. "Here's our old friend Hachiman," he said, "whom you half fancied might have had something to do with the tragedy. Well, you were right. Hachiman had a good deal to do with it, and with the various disasters at Copleston's too. I will show you how."

The figure, which was larger than life-size, had been set up temporarily on a large packing-case, hidden by a red cloth covering. Hachiman was represented in the familiar Japanese kneeling-sitting position, and the carving of the whole thing was of an intricate and close description. The god was represented as clad in ancient armour, with a large and loose cloak depending from his shoulders and falling behind in a wilderness of marvellously and deeply carved folds.

"See here," Dorrington said, placing his fingers under a projecting part of the base of the figure, and motioning to Mr. Colson to do the same. "Lift. Pretty heavy, eh?"

The idol was, indeed, enormously heavy, and it must have required the exertions of several strong men to place it where it was. "It seems pretty solid, doesn't it?" Dorrington continued. "But look here." He stepped to the back of the image, and, taking a prominent fold of the cloak in one hand, with a quick pull and a simultaneous rap of the other fist two feet above, a great piece of the carved drapery lifted on a hinge near the shoulders, displaying a hollow interior. In a dark corner within a small bottle and a fragment of rag were just visible.

"See there," said Dorrington, "there wouldn't be enough room in there for you or me, but a small man—a Japanese priest of the old time, say—could squat pretty comfortably. And see!"—he pointed to a small metal bolt at the bottom of the swing drapery—"he could bolt himself safely in when he got there. Whether the priest went there to play the oracle, or to blow fire out of Hachiman's mouth and nose I don't know, though no doubt it might be an interesting subject for inquiry; perhaps he did both. You observe the chamber is lined with metal, which does something towards giving the thing its weight, and there are cunning little openings among the armour-joints in front which would transmit air and sound—even permit of a peep out. Now Mr. Deacon might or might not have found out this back door after the figure had been a while in his possession, but it is certain he knew nothing of it when he bought it. Copleston knew nothing of it, though the thing has stood in his place for months. You see it's not a thing one would notice at once—I never should have done so if I hadn't been looking for it." He shut the part, and the joints, of irregular outline, fell into the depths of the folds, and vanished as if by magic.

"Now," Dorrington went on, "as I told you, Copleston knew nothing of this, but one of his men found it out. Do you happen to have heard of one Samuel Castro, nicknamed 'Slackjaw,' a hunchback whom Copleston employed on odd jobs?"

"I have seen him here. He called, sometimes with messages, sometimes with parcels. I should probably have forgotten all about him were it not that he was rather an extraordinary creature, even among Copleston's men, who are all remarkable. But did he—"

"He murdered Mr. Deacon, I think," Dorrington replied, "as I fancy I can explain to you. But he won't hang for it, for he was drowned this afternoon before my eyes, in an attempt to escape from the police. He was an extraordinary creature, as you have said. He wasn't English—a half-caste of some sort I think—though his command of language, of the riverside and dock description, was very free; it got him his nickname of Slackjaw among the longshoremen. He was desperately excitable, and he had most of the vices, though I don't think he premeditated murder in this case—nothing but robbery. He was immensely strong, although such a little fellow, and sharp in his wits, and he might have had regular work at Copleston's if he had liked, but that wasn't his game—he was too lazy. He would work long enough to earn a shilling or so, and then he would go off to drink the money. So he was a sort of odd on-and-off man at Copleston's—just to run a message or carry something or what not when the regular men were busy. Well, he seems to have been smart enough—or perhaps it was no more than an accident—to find out about Hachiman's back, and he used his knowledge for his own purposes. Copleston couldn't account for missing things in the night—because he never guessed that Castro, by shutting himself up in Hachiman about closing time, had the run of the place when everybody had gone, and could pick up any trifle that looked suitable for the pawnshop in the morning. He could sleep comfortably on sacks or among straw, and thus save the rent of lodgings, and he could accept Hachiman's shelter again just before Copleston turned up to start the next day's business. Getting out, too, after the place was opened, was quite easy, for nobody came to the large store-rooms till something was wanted, and in a large place with many doors and gates, like Copleston's, unperceived going and coming was easy to one who knew the ropes. So that Slackjaw would creep quietly out, and in again by the front door to ask for a job. Copleston noticed how regular he had been every morning for the past few months, and thought he was getting steadier! As to the things that got smashed, I expect Slackjaw knocked them over, getting out in the dark. One china vase, in particular, had been shifted at the last moment, probably after he was in his hiding-place, and stood behind the image. That was smashed, of course. And these things, coming after the bad voyage of the ship in which he came over, very naturally gave poor Hachiman an unlucky reputation.

"Probably Slackjaw was sorry at first when he heard that Hachiman was bought. But then an idea struck him. He had been to Mr. Deacon's rooms on errands, and must have seen that fine old plate in the sitting-room. He had picked up unconsidered trifles at Copleston's by aid of Hachiman—why not acquire something handsome at Deacon's in the same way? The figure was to be carried to Bedford Mansions as soon as work began on Wednesday morning. Very well. All he had to do was to manage his customary sojourn at Copleston's over Tuesday night, and keep to his hiding-place in the morning. He did it. Perhaps the men swore a bit at the weight of Hachiman, but as the idol weighed several hundredweights by itself, and had not been shifted since it first arrived, they most likely perceived no difference. Hachiman, with Slackjaw comfortably bolted inside him (though even *he* must have found the quarters narrow) jolted away in the waggon, and in course of time was deposited where it now stands.

"Of course all I have told you, and all I am about to tell you, is no more than conjecture—but I think you will say I have reasons. From within the idol Slackjaw could hear Mr. Deacon's movements, and no doubt when he heard him take his hat and stick and shut the outer door behind him, Hachiman's tenant was glad to get out. He had never had so long and trying a sojourn in the idol before, though he *had* provided himself this time with something to keep his spirits up—in that little flat bottle he left behind. Probably, however, he waited some little time before emerging, for safety's sake. I judge this because I found no signs of his having started work, except a single small knife-mark on the plate case. He must have no more than begun when Mr. Deacon came back for his letters. First, however, he went and shut the bedroom window, lest his movements might be heard in some adjacent rooms; the man who was painting said he heard that, you remember. Well, hearing Mr. Deacon's key in the lock, of course he made a rush for his hiding-place—but there was no time to get in and close up before Mr. Deacon could hear the noise. Mr. Deacon, as he entered, heard the footsteps in the next room, and went to see. The result you know. Castro, perhaps, crouched behind the idol, and hearing Mr. Deacon approaching, and knowing discovery inevitable, in his mad fear and excitement, snatched the nearest weapon and struck wildly at his pursuer. See! here are half a dozen heavy, short Japanese swords at hand, any one of which might have been used. The thing done, Castro had to think of escape. The door was impossible—the hall-porter was already knocking there. But the man had no key—he could be heard moving about and calling for one. There was yet a little time. He wiped the blade of the weapon, put it back in its place, took the keys from the dead man's pocket, and regained his concealment in the idol. Whether or not he took the keys with the idea of again attempting theft when the room was left empty I don't know—most likely he thought they would aid him in escape. Anyway, he didn't attempt theft, but lay in his concealment—and a pretty bad time he must have had of it—till night. Probably his nerve was not good enough for anything more than simple flight. When all was quiet, he left the rooms and shut the door behind him. Then he lurked about corridors and basements till morning, and when the doors were opened, slipped out unobserved. That's all. It's pretty obvious, once you know about Hachiman's interior."

"And how did you find out?"

"When you left me here I considered the thing. I put aside all suspicions of motive, the Japanese and his sword and the rest of it, and addressed myself to the bare facts. Somebody *had* been in these rooms when Mr. Deacon came back, and that somebody had murdered him. The first thing was to find how this person came, and where he came from. At first, of course, one thought of the bedroom window, as the police had done. But reflection proved this unlikely. Mr. Deacon had entered his front door, was inside a few seconds, and then was murdered close by the figure of Hachiman. Now if anybody had entered by the window for purposes of robbery, his impulse on hearing the key in the outer door (and such a thing could be heard all over the rooms, as I tested for myself)—his impulse, I say, would be to retreat by the way he had come, that is by the window. If, then, Mr. Deacon had overtaken him before he could escape, the murder might have taken place just as it had done, but it would have been *in the bedroom*, not in a room in the opposite direction. And any thief's attention would naturally be directed at first to the gold plate—indeed, I detected a fresh knife-mark in the door of the case, which I will show you presently. Now, as you see by the arrangement of the rooms, the retreat from the plate case to the bedroom window would be a short one, whereas the murderer must in fact have taken a longer journey in the opposite direction. Why?

Because he had *arrived* from that direction, and his natural impulse was to retreat by the way he had come. This might have been by the door to the back stairs, but a careful examination of this door and its lock and key convinced me that it had not been opened. The key was dirty, and to have turned it from the opposite side would have necessitated the forcible use of a pair of thin hollow pliers (a familiar tool to burglars), and these must have left their mark on the dirty key. So I turned back to the idol. *This* was the spot the intruder had made for in his retreat, and the figure had been brought into the place the very morning of the murder. Also, things had disappeared from its vicinity at Copleston's. More—it was a large thing. What if it were hollow? One has heard of such things having been invented by priests anxious for certain effects. Could not a thief smuggle himself in that way?

"The suggestion was a little startling, for if it were the right one the man might be hiding there at that moment. I gave the thing half an hour's examination, and in the end found what I have shown you. It was not the sort of thing one would have found out without looking for it. Look at it even now. Although you have seen it open, you couldn't point to the joints."

Dorrington opened it again. "Once open," he went on, "the thing was pretty plain. Here is the rag—perhaps it was Castro's pocket-handkerchief—used to wipe the weapon. It is stained all over, and cut, as you will observe, by the sharp edge. Also, you may see a crumb or two—Slackjaw had brought food with him, in case of a long imprisonment. But chiefly observe the bottle. It is a flat, high-shouldered, 'quartern' bottle, such as publicans sell or lend to their customers in poor districts, and as usual it bears the publican's name—J. Mills. It's a most extraordinary thing, but it seems the fate of almost every murderer, no matter how cunning, to leave some such damning piece of evidence about, foolish as it may seem afterward. I've known it in a dozen cases. Probably Castro, in the dark and in his excitement, forgot it when he quitted his hiding-place. At any rate it helped me and made my course plain. Clearly this man, whoever he was, had come from Copleston's. Moreover, he was a small man, for the space he had occupied would be too little even for a man of middle height. Also he bought drink of J. Mills, a publican; if J. Mills carried on business near Copleston's so much the easier my task would seem. Before I left, however, I went to the basement and inspected the ladder, the removal of which had caused the police so much exercise. Then it was plain why Dowden had cleared out. All his prevarication and uneasiness were explained at once, as the police might have seen if they had looked *behind* the ladder as well as at it. For it had been lying lengthwise against the wooden partition which formed the back of the compartments put up to serve the tenants as wine-cellars. Dowden had taken three planks out of this partition, and so arranged that they could be slipped in their places and out again without attracting attention. What he had been taking through the holes he thus made I won't undertake to say, but I will make a small bet that some of the tenants find their wine short presently! And so Dowden, never an industrious person, and never at one job long, thought it best to go away when he found the police asking why the ladder had been moved."

"Yes, yes—it's very surprising, but no doubt you're right. Still, what about Kanamaro and that sword?"

"Tell me exactly what he said to you to-day."

Mr. Colson detailed the conversation at length.

Dorrington smiled. "See here," he said, "I have found out something else in these rooms. What Kanamaro said he meant in another sense to what you supposed. *I* wondered a little about that sword, and made a little search among some drawers in consequence. Look here. Do you see this box standing out here on a nest of drawers? That is quite unlike Mr. Deacon's orderly ways. The box contains a piece of lacquer, and it had been shifted from its drawer to make room for a more precious piece. See here." Dorrington pulled out a drawer just below where the box stood, and took from it another white wood box. He opened this box and removed a quantity of wadding. A rich brocade *fukusa* was then revealed, and, loosening the cord of this, Dorrington displayed a Japanese writing-case, or *suzuribako*, aged and a little worn at the corners, but all of lacquer of a beautiful violet hue.

"What!" exclaimed Mr. Colson. "Violet lacquer!"

"That is what it is," Dorrington answered, "and when I saw it I judged at once that Deacon had at last consented to part with his Masamuné blade in exchange for that even greater rarity, a fine piece of the real old violet lacquer. I should imagine that Kanamaro brought it on Tuesday evening—you will remember that you saw Mr. Deacon for the last time alive in the afternoon of that day. Beard seems not to have noticed him, but in the evening hall-porters are apt to be at supper, you know—perhaps even taking a nap now and then!"

"Then *this* is how Kanamaro 'finished his business'!" Mr. Colson observed. "And the 'very great cost' was probably what he had to pay for this."

"I suppose so. And he would not have believed it possible that he *could* get a piece of violet lacquer in any circumstances."

"But," Mr. Colson objected, "I still don't understand his indifference and lack of surprise when I told him of poor Deacon's death."

"I think that is very natural in such a man as Keigo Kanamaro. I don't profess to know a very great deal about Japan, but I know that a *samurai* of the old school was trained from infancy to look on death, whether his own or another's, with absolute indifference. They regarded it as a mere circumstance. Consider how cold-bloodedly their *hari-kiri*, their legalised suicide, was carried out!"

As they left the rooms and made for the street Mr. Colson said, "But now I know nothing of your pursuit of Castro."

Dorrington shrugged his shoulders. "There is little to say," he said. "I went to Copleston and asked him if any one of his men was missing all day on Wednesday. None of his regular men were, it seemed, but he had seen nothing that day of an odd man named Castro, or Slackjaw, although he had been very regular for some time before; and, indeed, Castro had not yet turned up. I asked if Castro was a tall man. No, he was a little fellow and a hunchback, Copleston told me. I asked what public-house one might find him at, and Copleston mentioned the 'Blue Anchor'—kept, as I had previously ascertained from the directory, by J. Mills. That was enough. With everything standing as it was, a few minutes' talk with the inspector in charge at the nearest police-station was all that was necessary. Two men were sent to make the arrest, and the people at the 'Blue Anchor' directed us to Martin's Wharf, where we found Castro. He had been drinking, but he knew enough to make a bolt the moment he saw the policemen coming on the wharf. He dropped on to a dummy barge and made off from one barge to another in what seemed an aimless direction, though he may have meant to get away at the stairs a little lower down the river. But he never got as far. He muddled one jump and fell between the barges. You know what a suck under there is when a man falls among barges like that. A strong swimmer with all his senses has only an off chance, and a man with bad whisky in his head—well, I left them dragging for Slackjaw when I came away."

As they turned the corner of the street they met a newsboy running. "Paper—speshal!" he cried. "The West-End murder—speshal! Suicide of the murderer!"

Dorrington's conjecture that Kanamaro had called to make his exchange on Tuesday evening proved correct. Mr. Colson saw him once more on the day of his departure, and told him the whole story. And then Keigo Kanamaro sailed for Japan to lay the sword in his father's tomb.

VI

Old Cater's Money

I

THE FIRM OF DORRINGTON & Hicks had not been constructed at
the time when this case came to Dorrington's hand. Dorrington had
barely emerged from the obscurity that veils his life before some ten
years ago, and he was at this time a needier adventurer than he had
been at the period of any other of the cases I have related. Indeed, his
illicit gains on this occasion would seem first to have set him on his feet
and enabled him first to cut a fair exterior figure. Whether or not
he had developed to the full the scoundrelism that first brought me
acquainted with his trade I do not know; but certain it is that he was
involved at the time in transactions wretchedly ill paid, on behalf of
one Flint, a shipstores dealer at Deptford; an employer whose record
was never a very clean one. This Flint was one of an unpleasant family.
He was nephew to old Cater the wharfinger (and private usurer) and
cousin to another Cater, whose name was Paul, and who was also a
usurer, though he variously described himself as a "commission agent"
or "general dealer." Indeed, he was a general dealer, if the term may be
held to include a dealer in whatever would bring him gain, and who
made no great punctilio in regard to the honesty or otherwise of his
transactions. In fact, all three of these pleasant relatives had records of
the shadiest, and all three did whatever in the way of money-lending,
mortgaging, and blood-sucking came in their way. It is, however, with
old Cater—Jerry Cater, he was called—that this narrative is in the first
place concerned. I got the story from a certain Mr. Sinclair, who for
many years acted as his clerk and debt-collector.

Old Jerry Cater lived in the crooked and decaying old house over
his wharf by Bermondsey Wall, where his father had lived before him.
It was a grim and strange old house, with long-shut loft-doors in upper
floors, and hinged flaps in sundry rooms that, when lifted, gave startling
glimpses of muddy water washing among rotten piles below. Not once
in six months now did a barge land its load at Cater's Wharf, and no
coasting brig ever lay alongside. For, in fact, the day of Cater's Wharf

was long past; and it seemed indeed that few more days were left for old Jerry Cater himself. For seventy-eight years old Jerry Cater had led a life useless to himself and to everybody else, though his own belief was that he had profited considerably. Truly if one counted nothing but the money the old miser had accumulated, then his profit was large indeed; but it had brought nothing worth having, neither for himself nor for others, and he had no wife nor child who might use it more wisely when he should at last leave it behind him; no other relative indeed than his two nephews, each in spirit a fair copy of himself, though in body a quarter of a century younger. Seventy-eight years of every mean and sordid vice and of every virtue that had pecuniary gain for its sole object left Jerry Cater stranded at last in his cheap iron bedstead with its insufficient coverings, with not a sincere friend in the world to sit five minutes by his side. Down below, Sinclair, his unhappy clerk, had the accommodation of a wooden table and a chair; and the clerk's wife performed what meagre cooking and cleaning service old Cater would have. Sinclair was a man of forty-five, rusty, starved, honest, and very cheap. He was very cheap because it had been his foolishness, twenty years ago, when in City employ, to borrow forty pounds of old Cater to get married with, and to buy furniture, together with forty pounds he had of his own. Sinclair was young then, and knew nothing of the ways of the two hundred per cent. money-lender. When he had, by three or four years' pinching, paid about a hundred and fifty pounds on account of interest and fines, and only had another hundred or two still due to clear everything off, he fell sick and lost his place. The payment of interest ceased, and old Jerry Cater took his victim's body, soul, wife, sticks, and chairs together. Jerry Cater discharged his own clerk, and took Sinclair, with a saving of five shillings a week on the nominal salary, and out of the remainder he deducted, on account of the debt and ever-accumulating interest, enough to keep his man thin and broken-spirited, without absolutely incapacitating him from work, which would have been bad finance. But the rest of the debt, capital and interest, was made into a capital debt, with usury on the whole. So that for sixteen years or more Sinclair had been paying something every week off the eternally increasing sum, and might have kept on for sixteen centuries at the same rate without getting much nearer freedom. If only there had been one more room in the house old Cater might have compulsorily lodged his clerk, and have deducted something more for rent. As it was he might have used the office for the purpose, but he could never have brought himself to charge a small rent for it, and a large one would have swallowed most of the rest of Sinclair's salary, thus bringing him below starvation point, and impairing his working capacity. But Mrs. Sinclair, now gaunt and scraggy, did all the housework, so that that came very cheap. Most of the house was filled with old bales and rotting merchandise which old Jerry Cater had seized in payment for wharfage dues and other debts, and had held to, because his ideas of selling prices were large, though his notion of buying prices were small. Sinclair was out of doors more than in, dunning and threatening debtors as hopeless as himself. And the household was completed by one Samuel Greer, a squinting man of grease and rags, within ten years of the age of old Jerry Cater himself. Greer was wharf-hand, messenger, and personal attendant on his employer, and, with less opportunity, was thought to be near as bad a scoundrel as Cater. He lived and slept in the house, and was popularly supposed to be paid nothing at all; though his patronage of the "Ship and Anchor," hard by, was as frequent as might be.

Old Jerry Cater was plainly not long for this world. Ailing for months, he at length gave in and took to his bed. Greer watched him anxiously and greedily, for it was his design, when his master went at last, to get what he could for himself. More than once during his illness old Cater had sent Greer to fetch his nephews. Greer had departed on these errands, but never got farther than the next street. He hung about a reasonable time—perhaps in the "Ship and Anchor," if funds permitted—and then returned to say that the nephews could not come just yet. Old Cater had quarrelled with his nephews, as he had with everybody else, some time before, and Greer was resolved, if he could, to prevent any meeting now, for that would mean that the nephews would take possession of the place, and he would lose his chance of convenient larceny when the end came. So it was that neither nephew knew of old Jerry Cater's shaky condition.

Before long, finding that the old miser could not leave his bed— indeed he could scarcely turn in it—Greer took courage, in Sinclair's absence, to poke about the place in search of concealed sovereigns. He had no great time for this, because Jerry Cater seemed to have taken a great desire for his company, whether for the sake of his attendance or to keep him out of mischief was not clear. At any rate Greer found no concealed sovereigns, nor anything better than might be sold for a few pence at the ragshop. Until one day, when old Cater was taking alternate fits of restlessness and sleep, Greer ventured to take down a dusty old pickle-jar from the top shelf in the cupboard of his master's bedroom. Cater was dozing at the moment, and Greer, tilting the jar toward the light, saw within a few doubled papers, very dusty. He snatched the papers out, stuffed them into his pocket, replaced the jar, and closed the cupboard door hastily. The door made some little noise, and old Cater turned and woke, and presently he made a shift to sit up in bed, while Greer scratched his head as innocently as he could, and directed his divergent eyes to parts of the room as distant from the cupboard as possible.

"Sam'l Greer," said old Cater in a feeble voice, while his lower jaw waggled and twitched, "Sam'l Greer, I think I'll 'ave some beef-tea." He groped tremulously under his pillow, turning his back to Greer, who tiptoed and glared variously over his master's shoulders. He saw nothing, however, though he heard the chink of money. Old Cater turned, with a shilling in his shaking hand. "Git 'alf a pound o' shin o' beef," he said, "an' go to Green's for it at the other end o' Grange Road, d'ye hear? It's—it's a penny a pound cheaper there than it is anywhere nearer, and—and I ain't in so much of a 'urry for it, so the distance don't matter. Go 'long." And old Jerry Cater subsided in a fit of coughing.

Greer needed no second bidding. He was anxious to take a peep at the papers he had secreted. Sinclair was out collecting, or trying to collect, but Greer did not stop to examine his prize before he had banged the street door behind him, lest Cater, listening above, should wonder what detained him. But in a convenient courtyard a hundred yards away he drew out the papers and inspected them eagerly. First, there was the policy of insurance of the house and premises. Then there was a bundle of receipts for the yearly insurance premiums. And then—there was old Jerry Cater's will.

There were two foolscap sheets, written all in Jerry Cater's own straggling handwriting. Greer hastily scanned the sheets, and his dirty face grew longer and his squint intensified as he turned over the second sheet, found nothing behind it, and stuffed the papers back in his pocket. For it was plain that not a penny of old Jerry Cater's money was for his faithful servant, Samuel Greer. "Ungrateful ole waga-bone!" mused the faithful servant as he went his way. "Not a blessed 'a'peny; not a 'a'peny! An' them as don't want it gets it, o' course. That's always the way—it's like a-greasing' of a fat pig. I shall 'ave to get what I can while I can, that's all." And so ruminating he pursued his way to the butcher's in Grange Road.

Once more on his way there, and twice on his way back, Samuel Greer stepped into retired places to look at those papers again, and at each inspection he grew more thoughtful. There might be money in it yet. Come, he must think it over.

The front door being shut, and Sinclair probably not yet returned, he entered the house by a way familiar to the inmates—a latched door giving on to the wharf. The clock told him that he had been gone nearly an hour, but Sinclair was still absent. When he entered old Cater's room upstairs he found a great change. The old man lay in a state of collapse, choking with a cough that exhausted him; and for this there seemed little wonder, for the window was open, and the room was full of the cold air from the river.

"Wot jer bin openin' the winder for?" asked Greer in astonishment. "It's enough to give ye yer death." He shut it and returned to the bedside. But though he offered his master the change from the shilling the old man seemed not to see it nor to hear his voice.

"Well, if you won't—don't," observed Greer with some alacrity, pocketing the coppers. "But I'll bet he'll remember right enough presently." "D'y'ear," he added, bending over the bed, "I've got the beef. Shall I bile it now?"

But old Jerry Cater's eyes still saw nothing and he heard not, though his shrunken chest and shoulders heaved with the last shudders of the cough that had exhausted him. So Greer stepped lightly to the cupboard and restored the fire policy and the receipts to the pickle-jar. He kept the will.

Greer made preparations for cooking the beef, and as he did so he encountered another phenomenon. "Well, he have bin a goin' of it!" said Greer. "Blow me if he ain't bin readin' the Bible now!"

A large, ancient, worn old Bible, in a rough calf-skin cover, lay on a chair by old Cater's hand. It had probably been the family Bible of the Caters for generations back, for certainly old Jerry Cater would never have bought such a thing. For many years it had accumulated dust on a distant shelf among certain out-of-date account-books, but Greer had never heard of its being noticed before. "Feels he goin', that's about it," Greer mused as he pitched the Bible back on the shelf to make room for his utensils. "But I shouldn't ha' thought 'e'd take it sentimental like that—readin' the Bible an' lettin' in the free air of 'eaven to make 'im cough 'isself blind."

The beef-tea was set simmering, and still old Cater lay impotent. The fit of prostration was longer than any that had preceded it, and presently Greer thought it might be well to call the doctor. Call him he did accordingly (the surgery was hard by), and the doctor came. Jerry Cater revived a little, sufficiently to recognise the doctor, but it was his last effort. He lived another hour and a half. Greer kept the change and had the beef-tea as well. The doctor gave his opinion that the old man had risen in delirium and had expended his last strength in moving about the room and opening the window.

II

SAMUEL GREER FOUND SOMEWHERE NEAR two pounds in silver in the small canvas bag under the dead man's pillow. No more money, however, rewarded his hasty search about the bedroom, and when Sinclair returned Greer set off to carry the news to Paul Cater, the dead man's nephew.

The respectable Greer had considered well the matter of the will, and saw his way, he fancied, at least to a few pounds by way of compensation for his loss of employment and the ungrateful forgetfulness of his late employer. The two sheets comprised, in fact, not a simple will merely, but a will and a codicil, each on one of the sheets, the codicil being a year or two more recent than the will. Nobody apparently knew anything of these papers, and it struck Greer that it was now in his power to prevent anybody learning, unless an interested party were disposed to pay for the disclosure. That was why he now took his way toward the establishment of Paul Cater, for the will made Paul Cater not only sole executor, but practically sole legatee. Wherefore Greer carefully separated the will from the codicil, intending the will alone for sale to Paul Cater. Because, indeed, the codicil very considerably modified it, and might form the subject of independent commerce.

Paul Cater made a less miserly show than had been the wont of his uncle. His house was in a street in Pimlico, the ground-floor front room of which was made into an office, with a wire blind carrying his name in gilt letters. Perhaps it was that Paul Cater carried his covetousness to a greater refinement than his uncle had done, seeing that a decent appearance is a commercial advantage by itself, bringing a greater profit than miserly habits could save.

The man of general dealings was balancing his books when Greer arrived, but at the announcement of his uncle's death he dropped everything. He was not noticeably stricken with grief, unless a sudden seizure of his hat and a roaring aloud for a cab might be considered as indications of affliction; for in truth Paul Cater knew well that it was a case in which much might depend on being first at Bermondsey Wall. The worthy Greer had scarce got the news out before he found himself standing in the street while Cater was giving directions to a cabman. "Here—you come in too," said Cater, and Greer was bustled into the cab.

It was plainly a situation in which half-crowns should not be too reluctantly parted with. So Paul Cater produced one and presented it. Cater was a strong-faced man of fifty odd, with a tight-drawn mouth that proclaimed everywhere a tight fist; so that the unaccustomed passing over of a tip was a noticeably awkward and unspontaneous performance, and Greer pocketed the money with little more acknowledgment than a growl.

"Do you know where he put the will?" asked Paul Cater with a keen glance.

"Will?" answered Greer, looking him blankly in the face—the gaze of one eye passing over Cater's shoulder and that of the other seeming to seek his boots. "Will? P'raps 'e never made one."

"Didn't he?"

"That 'ud mean, lawfully, as the property would come to you an' Mr. Flint—'arves. Bein' all personal property. So I'd think." And Greer's composite gaze blankly persisted.

"But how do you know whether he made a will or not?"

"'Ow do I know? Ah, well, p'raps I dunno. It's only fancy like. I jist put it to you—that's all. It 'ud be divided atween the two of you." Then, after a long pause, he added: "But lor! it 'ud be a pretty fine thing for you if he did leave a will, and willed it all to you, wouldn't it? Mighty fine thing! An' it 'ud be a mighty fine thing for Mr. Flint if there was a will leaving it all to him, wouldn't it? Pretty fine thing!"

Cater said nothing, but watched Greer's face sharply. Greer's face, with its greasy features and its irresponsible squint, was as expressive as a brick. They travelled some distance in silence. Then Greer said musingly, "Ah, a will like that 'ud be a mighty fine thing! What 'ud you be disposed to give for it now?"

"Give for it? What do you mean? If there's a will there's an end to it. Why should I give anything for it?"

"Jist so—jist so," replied Greer, with a complacent wave of the hand. "Why should you? No reason at all, unless you couldn't find it without givin' something."

"See here, now," said Cater sharply, "let us understand this. Do you mean that there is a will, and you know that it is hidden, and where it is?"

Greer's squint remained impenetrable. "Hidden? Lor!—'ow should I know if it was hidden? I was a-puttin' of a case to you."

"Because," Cater went on, disregarding the reply, "if that's the case, the sooner you out with the information the better it'll be for you. Because there are ways of making people give up information of that sort for nothing."

"Yes—o' course," replied the imperturbable Greer. "O' course there is. An' quite right too. Ah, it's a fine thing is the lawr—a mighty fine thing!"

The cab rattled over the stones of Bermondsey Wall, and the two alighted at the door through which old Jerry Cater was soon to come feet first. Sinclair was back, much disturbed and anxious. At sight of Paul Cater the poor fellow, weak and broken-spirited, left the house as quietly as he might. For years of grinding habit had inured him to the belief that in reality old Cater had treated him rather well, and now he feared the probable action of the heirs.

"Who was that?" asked Paul Cater of Greer. "Wasn't it the clerk that owed my uncle the money?"

Greer nodded.

"Then he's not to come here again—do you hear? I'll take charge of the books and things. As to the debt—well, I'll see about that after. And now look here." Paul Cater stood before Greer and spoke with decision. "About that will, now. Bring it."

Greer was not to be bluffed. "Where from?" he asked innocently.

"Will you stand there and tell me you don't know where it is?"

"Maybe I'd best stand here and tell you what pays me best."

"Pay you? How much more do you want? Bring me that will, or I'll have you in gaol for stealing it!"

"Lor!" answered Greer composedly, conscious of holding another trump as well as the will. "Why, if there *was* anybody as knowed where the will was, and you talked to him as violent as that 'ere, why, you'd frighten him so much he'd as likely as not go out and get a price from your cousin, Mr. Flint. Whatever was in the will it might pay him to get hold of it."

At this moment there came a furious knocking at the front door. "Why," Greer continued, "I bet that's him. It can't be nobody else—I bet the doctor's told him, or summat."

They were on the first-floor landing, and Greer peeped from a broken-shuttered window that looked on the street. "Yes," he said, "that's Mr. Flint sure enough. Now, Mr. Paul Cater, business. Do you want to see that will before I let Mr. Flint in?"

"Yes!" exclaimed Cater furiously, catching at his arm. "Quick— where is it?"

"I want twenty pound."

"Twenty pound! You're mad! What for?"

"All right, if I'm mad, I'll go an' let Mr. Flint in."

The knocking was repeated, louder and longer.

"No," cried Cater, getting in his way. "You know you mustn't conceal a will—that's law. Give it up."

"What's the law that says I must give it up to you, 'stead of yer cousin? *If* there's a will it may say anythin'—in yer favour or out of it. If there ain't, you'll git 'alf. The will might give you more, or it might give you less, or it might give you nothink. Twenty pound for first look at it 'fore Flint comes in, and do what you like with it 'fore he knows anythink about it."

Again the knocking came at the door, this time supplemented by kicks.

"But I don't carry twenty pound about with me!" protested Cater, waving his fists. "Give me the will and come to my office for the money to-morrow!"

"No tick for this sort of job," answered Greer decisively. "Sorry I can't oblige you—I'm goin' down to the front door." And he made as though to go.

"Well, look here!" said Cater desperately, pulling out his pocket-book. "I've got a note or two, I think—"

"'Ow much?" asked Greer, calmly laying hold of the pocket-book. "Two at least. Two fivers. Well, I'll let it go at that. Give us hold." He took the notes, and pulled out the will from his pocket. Flint, outside, battered the door once more.

"Why," exclaimed Cater as he glanced over the sheet, "I'm sole executor and I get the lot! Who are these witnesses?"

"Oh, they're all right. Longshore hands just hereabout. You'll get 'em any day at the 'Ship and Anchor.'"

Cater put the will in his breast-pocket. "You'd best get out o' this, my man," he said. "You've had me for ten pound, and the further you get from me the safer you'll be."

"What?" said Greer with a chuckle. "Not even grateful! Shockin'!" He took his way downstairs, and Cater followed. At the door Flint, a counterpart of Cater, except that his dress was more slovenly, stood ragefully.

"Ah, cousin," said Cater, standing on the threshold and preventing his entrance, "this is a very sad loss!"

"Sad loss!" Flint replied with disgust. "A lot you think of the loss—as much as I do, I reckon. I want to come in."

"Then you sha'n't!" Cater replied, with a prompt change of manner. "You shan't! I'm sole executor, and I've got the will in my pocket." He pulled it out sufficiently far to show the end of the paper, and then returned it. "As executor I'm in charge of the property, and responsible. It's vested in me till the will's put into effect. That's law. And it's a bad thing for anybody to interfere with an executor. That's law too."

Flint was angry, but cautious. "Well," he said, "you're uncommon high, with your will and your executor's law and your 'sad loss,' I must say. What's your game?"

For answer Cater began to shut the door.

"Just you look out!" cried Flint. "You haven't heard the last of this! You may be executor or it may be a lie. You may have the will or you may not; anyway I know better than to run the risk of putting myself in the wrong now. But I'll watch you, and I'll watch this house, and I'll be about when the will comes to be proved! And if that ain't done quick, I'll apply for administration myself, and see the thing through!"

III

SAMUEL GREER SHEERED OFF AS the cousinly interview ended, well satisfied with himself. Ten pounds was a fortune to him, and he meant having a good deal more. He did nothing further till the following morning, when he presented himself at the shop of Jarvis Flint.

"Good mornin', Mr. Flint," said Samuel Greer, grinning and squinting affably. "I couldn't help noticin' as you had a few words yesterday with Mr. Cater after the sad loss."

"Well?"

"It 'appens as I've seen the will as Mr. Cater was talkin' of, an' I thought p'raps it 'ud save you makin' mistakes if I told you of it."

"What about it?" Jarvis Flint was not disposed to accept Greer altogether on trust.

"Well it *do* seem a scandalous thing, certainly, but what Mr. Cater said was right. He *do* take the personal property, subjick to debts, an' he do take the freehold prim'ses. An' he is the 'xecutor."

"Was the will witnessed?"

"Yes—two waterside chaps well know'd there-abouts."

"Was it made by a lawyer?"

"No—all in the lamented corpse's 'andwritin'."

"Umph!" Flint maintained his hard stare in Greer's face. "Anything else?"

"Well, no, Mr. Flint, sir, p'raps not. But I wonder if there might be sich a thing as a codicil?"

"Is there?"

"Oh, I was a-wonderin', that's all. It might make a deal o' difference in the will, mightn't it? And p'raps Mr. Cater mightn't know anythink about the codicil."

"What do you mean? Is there a codicil?"

"Well, reely, Mr. Flint," answered Greer with a deprecatory grin— "reely it ain't business to give information for nothink, is it?"

"Business or not, if you know anything you'll find you'll have to tell it. I'm not going to let Cater have it all his own way, if he *is* executor. My lawyer'll be on the job before you're a day older, my man, and you won't find it pay to keep things too quiet."

"But it can't pay worse than to give information for nothink," persisted Greer. "Come, now, Mr. Flint, s'pose (I don't say there is, mind—I only say *s'pose*)—s'pose there *was* a codicil, and s'pose that codicil meant a matter of a few thousand pound in your pocket. And s'pose some person could tell you where to put your hand on that codicil, what might you be disposed to pay that person?"

"Bring me the codicil," answered Flint, "and if it's all right I'll give you—well, say five shillings."

Greer grinned again and shook his head. "No, reely, Mr. Flint," he said, "we can't do business on terms like them. Fifty pound down in my hand now, and it's done. Fifty 'ud be dirt cheap. And the longer you are a-considerin'—well, you know, Mr. Cater might get hold of it, and then, why, s'pose it got burnt and never 'eard of agen?"

Flint glared with round eyes. "You get out!" he said. "Go on! Fifty pound, indeed! Fifty pound, without my knowing whether you're telling lies or not! Out you go! I know what to do now, my man!"

Greer grinned once more, and slouched out. He had not expected to bring Flint to terms at once. Of course the man would drive him away at first, and, having got scent of the existence of the codicil, and supposing it to be somewhere concealed about the old house at Bermondsey Wall, he would set his lawyer to warn his cousin that the thing was known, and that he, as executor, would be held responsible for it. But the trump card, the codicil itself, was carefully stowed in the lining of Greer's hat, and Cater knew nothing about it. Presently Flint, finding Cater obdurate, would approach the wily Greer again, and then he could be squeezed. Meanwhile the hat-lining was as safe a place as any in which to keep the paper. Perhaps Flint might take a fancy to have him waylaid at night and searched, in which case a pocket would be an unsafe repository.

Flint, on his part, was in good spirits. Plainly there *was* a codicil, favourable to himself. Certainly he meant neither to pay Greer for discovering it—at any rate no such sum as fifty pounds—nor to abate a jot of his rights. Flint had a running contract with a shady solicitor, named Lugg, in accordance with which Lugg received a yearly payment and transacted all his legal business—consisting chiefly of writing threatening letters to unfortunate debtors. Also, as I think I have mentioned, Dorrington was working for him at the time, and working at very cheap rates. Flint resolved, to begin with, to set Dorrington and Lugg to work. But first Dorrington—who, as a matter of fact, was in Flint's back office during the interview with Greer. Thus it was that in an hour or two Dorrington found himself in active pursuit of Samuel Greer, with instructions to watch him closely, to make him drunk if possible, and to get at his knowledge of the codicil by any means conceivable.

IV

ON THE MORNING OF THE day after his talk with Flint, Samuel Greer ruminated doubtfully on the advisability of calling on the ship-store dealer again, or waiting in dignified silence till Flint should approach him. As he ruminated he rubbed his chin, and so rubbing it found it very stubbly. He resolved on the luxury of a penny shave, and, as he walked the street, kept his eyes open for a shop where the operation was performed at that price. Mr. Flint, at any rate, could wait till his chin was smooth. Presently, in a turning by Abbey Street, Bermondsey, he came on just such a barber's shop as he wanted. Within, two men were being shaved already, and another waiting; and Greer felt himself especially fortunate in that three more followed at his heels. He was ahead of their turns, anyhow. So he waited patiently.

The man whose turn was immediately before his own did not appear to be altogether sober. A hiccough shook him from time to time; he grinned with a dull glance at a comic paper held upside down in his hand, and when he went to take his turn at a chair his walk was unsteady. The barber had to use his skill to avoid cutting him, and he opened his mouth to make remarks at awkward times. Then Greer's turn came at the other chair, and when his shave was half completed he saw the unsteady customer rise, pay his penny, and go out.

"Beginnin' early in the mornin'!" observed one customer.

The barber laughed. "Yes," he said. "He wants to get a proper bust on before he goes to bed, I s'pose."

Samuel Greer's chin being smooth at last, he rose and turned to where he had hung his hat. His jaw dropped, and his eyes almost sprang out to meet each other as he saw—a bare peg! The unsteady customer had walked off with the wrong hat—his hat, and—the paper concealed inside!

"Lor!" cried the dismayed Greer, "he's took my hat!"

All the shopful of men set up a guffaw at this. "Take 'is then," said one. "It's a blame sight better one than yourn!"

But Greer, without a hat, rushed into the street, and the barber, without his penny, rushed after him. "Stop 'im!" shouted Greer distractedly. "Stop thief!"

Thus it was that Dorrington, at this time of a far less well-groomed appearance than was his later wont, watching outside the barber's, observed the mad bursting forth of Greer, followed by the barber. After the barber came the customers, one grinning furiously beneath a coating of lather.

"Stop 'im!" cried Greer. "'E's got my 'at! Stop 'im!"

"You pay me my money," said the barber, catching his arm. "Never mind yer 'at—you can 'ave 'is. But just you pay me first."

"Leave go! You're responsible for lettin' 'im take it, I tell you! It's a special 'at—valuable; leave go!"

Dorrington stayed to hear no more. Three minutes before he had observed a slightly elevated navvy emerge from the shop and walk solemnly across the street under a hat manifestly a size or two too small for him. Now Dorrington darted down the turning which the man had taken. The hat was a wretched thing, and there must be some special reason for Greer's wild anxiety to recover it, especially as the navvy must have left another, probably better, behind him. Already Dorrington had conjectured that Greer was carrying the codicil about with him, for he had no place else to hide it, and he would scarcely have offered so confidently to negotiate over it if it had been in the Bermondsey Wall house, well in reach of Paul Cater. So he followed the elevated navvy with all haste. He might never have seen him again were it not that the unconscious bearer of the fortunes of Flint (and, indeed, Dorrington) hesitated for a little while whether or not to enter the door of a public-house near St. Saviour's Dock. In the end he decided to go on, and it was just as he had started that Dorrington sighted him again.

The navvy walked slowly and gravely on, now and again with a swerve to the wall or the curb, but generally with a careful and laboured directness. Presently he arrived at a dock-bridge, with a low iron rail. An incoming barge attracted his eye, and he stopped and solemnly inspected it. He leaned on the low rail for this purpose, and as he did so the hat, all too small, fell off. Had he been standing two yards nearer the centre of the bridge it would have dropped into the water. As it was it fell on the quay, a few feet from the edge, and a dockman, coming toward the steps by the bridge-side, picked it up and brought it with him.

"Here y'are, mate," said the dockman, offering the hat.

The navvy took it in lofty silence, and inspected it narrowly. Then he said, "'Ere—wot's this? This ain't my 'at!" And he glared suspiciously at the dockman.

"Ain't it?" answered the dockman carelessly.

"Aw right then, keep it for the bloke it b'longs to. I don't want it."

"No," returned the navvy with rising indignation, "but I want mine, though! Wotcher done with it? Eh? It ain't a rotten old 'un like this 'ere. None o' yer 'alf-larks. Jist you 'and it over, come on!"

"'And wot over?" asked the dockman, growing indignant in his turn. "You drops yer 'at over the bridge like some kid as can't take care of it, and I brings it up for ye. 'Stead o' sayin' thank ye, 'like a man, y' asks me for another 'at! Go an' bile yer face!" And he turned on his heel.

"No, ye don't!" bawled the navvy, dropping the battered hat and making a complicated rush at the other's retreating form. "Not much! You gimme my 'at!" And he grabbed the dockman anywhere, with both hands.

The dockman was as big as the navvy, and no more patient. He immediately punched his assailant's nose; and in three seconds a mingled bunch of dockman and navvy was floundering about the street. Dorrington saw no more. He had the despised hat in his hand, and, general attention being directed to the action in progress, he hurried quietly up the nearest court.

V

Samuel Greer, having got clear of the barber by paying his penny, was in much perplexity, and this notwithstanding his acquisition of the navvy's hat, a very decent bowler, which covered his head generously and rested on his ears. What should be the move now? His hat was clean gone, and the codicil with it. To find it again would be a hopeless task, unless by chance the navvy should discover his mistake and return to the barber's to make a rectification of hats. So Samuel Greer returned once more to the barber's, and for the rest of the day called again and again fruitlessly. At first the barber was vastly amused, and told the story to his customers, who laughed. Then the barber got angry at the continual worrying, and at the close of the day's barbering he earned his night's repose by pitching Samuel Greer neck and crop into the gutter. Samuel Greer gathered himself up disconsolately, surrounded his head with the navvy's hat, and shuffled off to the "Ship and Anchor."

At the "Ship and Anchor" he found one Barker, a decayed and sodden lawyer's clerk out of work. Greer's temporary affluence enabling him to stand drinks, he was presently able, by putting artfully hypothetical cases, to extract certain legal information from Barker. Chiefly he learned that if a will or a codicil were missing, it might nevertheless be possible to obtain probate of it by satisfying the court with evidence of its contents and its genuineness. Here, at any rate, was a certain hope. He alone, apparently, of all persons, knew the contents of the codicil and the names of the witnesses; and since it was impossible to sell the codicil, now that it was gone, he might at least sell his evidence. He resolved to offer his evidence for sale to Flint at once, and take what he could get. There must be no delay, for possibly the navvy might find the paper in the hat and carry it to Flint, seeing that his name was beneficially mentioned in it, and his address given. Plainly the hat would not go back to the barber's now. If the drunken navvy had found out his mistake he probably had not the least notion where he had been nor where the hat had come from, else he would have returned it during the day, and recovered his own superior property. So Samuel Greer went at once, late as it was, and knocked up Mr. Flint.

Flint congratulated himself, feeling sure that Greer had thought better of his business and had come to give his information for anything he could get. Greer, on his part, was careful to conceal the fact that the codicil had been in his possession and had been lost. All he said was that he had seen the codicil, that its date was nine months later than that of the will, and that it benefited Jarvis Flint to the extent of some ten thousand pounds; leaving Flint to suppose, if he pleased, that Cater, the executor, had the codicil, but would probably suppress it. Indeed this was the conclusion that Flint immediately jumped at.

And the result of the interview was this: Flint, with much grudging and reluctance, handed over as a preliminary fee the sum of one pound, the most he could be screwed up to. Then it was settled that Greer should come on the morrow and consult with Flint and his solicitor Lugg, the object of the consultation being the construction of a consistent tale and a satisfactory *soi-disant* copy of the codicil, which Greer was to swear to, if necessary, and armed with which Paul Cater might be confronted and brought to terms.

It may be wondered why, ere this, Flint had not received the genuine codicil itself, recovered by Dorrington from Greer's hat. The fact was that Dorrington, as was his wont, was playing a little game of his own. Having possessed himself of the codicil, he was now in a position to make the most from both sides, and in a far more efficient manner than the clumsy Greer. People of Jarvis Flint's sordid character are apt, with all their sordid keenness, to be wonderfully short-sighted in regard to what might seem fairly obvious to a man of honest judgment. Thus it never occurred to Flint that a man like Dorrington, willing, for a miserable wage, to apply his exceptional subtlety to the furtherance of his employer's rascally designs, would be at least as ready to swindle that master on his own account when the opportunity offered; would be, in fact, the more ready, in proportion to the stinginess wherewith his master had treated him.

Having found the codicil, Dorrington's procedure was not to hand it over forthwith to Flint. It was this: first he made a careful and exact copy of the codicil; then he procured two men of his acquaintance, men of good credit, to read over the copy, word for word, and certify it as being an exact copy of the original by way of a signed declaration written on the back of the copy. Then he was armed at all points.

He packed the copy carefully away in his pocket-book, and with the original in his coat pocket, he called at the house in Bermondsey Wall, where Paul Cater had taken up his quarters to keep guard over everything till the will should be proved. So it happened that, while Samuel Greer, Jarvis Flint, and Lugg, the lawyer, were building their scheme, Dorrington was talking to Paul Cater at Cater's Wharf.

On the assurance that he had business of extreme importance, Cater took Dorrington into the room in which the old man had died. Cater was using this room as an office in which to examine and balance his uncle's books, and the corpse had been carried to a room below to await the funeral. Dorrington's clothes at this time, as I have hinted, were not distinguished by the excellence of cut and condition that was afterwards noticeable; in point of fact, he was seedy. But his assurance and his presence of mind were fully developed, and it was this very transaction that was to put the elegant appearance within his reach.

"Mr. Cater," he said, "I believe you are sole executor of the will of your uncle, Mr. Jeremiah Cater, who lived in this house." Cater assented.

"That will is one extremely favourable to yourself. In fact, by it you become not only sole executor, but practically sole legatee."

"Well?"

"I am here as a man of business and as a man of the world to give you certain information. There is a codicil to that will."

Cater started. Then he shrugged his shoulders and shook his head as though he knew better.

"There is a codicil," Dorrington went on, imperturbably, "executed in strict form, all in the handwriting of the testator, and dated nine months later than the will. That codicil benefits your cousin, Mr. Jarvis Flint, to the extent of ten thousand pounds. To put it in another way, it deprives *you* of ten thousand pounds."

Cater felt uneasy, but he did his best to maintain a contemptuous appearance. "You're rushing ahead pretty fast," he said, "talking about the terms of this codicil, as you call it. What I want to know is, where is it?"

"That," replied Dorrington, smilingly, "is a question very easily answered. The codicil is in my pocket." He tapped his coat as he spoke.

Paul Cater started again, and now he was plainly discomposed. "Very well," he said, with some bravado, "if you've got it you can show it to me, I suppose."

"Nothing easier," Dorrington responded affably. He stepped to the fireplace and took the poker. "You won't mind my holding the poker while you inspect the paper, will you?" he asked politely. "The fact is, the codicil is of such a nature that I fear a man of your sharp business instincts might be tempted to destroy it, there being no other witness present, unless you had the assurance (which I now give you) that if you as much as touch it I shall stun you with the poker. There is the codicil, which you may read with your hands behind you." He spread the paper out on the table, and Cater bent eagerly and read it, growing paler as his eye travelled down the sheet.

Before raising his eyes, however, he collected himself, and as he stood up he said, with affected contempt, "I don't care a brass farthing for this thing! It's a forgery on the face of it."

"Dear me!" answered Dorrington placidly, recovering the paper and folding it up; "that's very disappointing to hear. I must take it round to Mr. Flint and see if that is his opinion."

"No, you mustn't!" exclaimed Cater, desperately. "You say that's a genuine document. Very well. I'm still executor, and you are bound to give it to me."

"Precisely," Dorrington replied sweetly. "But in the strict interests of justice I think Mr. Flint, as the person interested, ought to have a look at it first, *in case* any accident should happen to it in your hands. Don't you?"

Cater knew he was in a corner, and his face betrayed it.

"Come," said Dorrington in a more business-like tone. "Here is the case in a nutshell. It is my business, just as it is yours, to get as much as I can for nothing. In pursuance of that business I quietly got hold of this codicil. Nobody but yourself knows I have it, and as to *how* I got it you needn't ask, for I sha'n't tell you. Here is the document, and it is worth ten thousand pounds to either of two people, yourself and Mr. Flint, your worthy cousin. I am prepared to sell it at a very great sacrifice—to sell it dirt cheap, in fact, and I give you the privilege of first refusal, for which you ought to be grateful. One thousand pounds is the price, and that gives you a profit of nine thousand pounds when you have destroyed the codicil—a noble profit of nine hundred per cent. at a stroke! Come, is it a bargain?"

"What?" exclaimed Cater, astounded. "A thousand pounds?"

"One thousand pounds exactly," replied Dorrington complacently, "and a penny for the receipt stamp—if you want a receipt."

"Oh," said Cater, "you're mad. A thousand pounds! Why, it's absurd!"

"Think so?" remarked Dorrington, reaching for his hat. "Then I must see if Mr. Flint agrees with you, that's all. He's a man of business, and I never heard of his refusing a certain nine hundred per cent. profit yet. Good-day!"

"No, stop!" yelled the desperate Cater. "Don't go. Don't be unreasonable now—say five hundred and I'll write you a cheque."

"Won't do," answered Dorrington, shaking his head. "A thousand is the price, and not a penny less. And not by cheque, mind. I understand all moves of that sort. Notes or gold. I wonder at a smart man like yourself expecting me to be so green."

"But I haven't the money here."

"Very likely not. Where's your bank? We'll go there and get it."

Cater, between his avarice and his fears, was at his wits' end. "Don't be so hard on me, Mr. Dorrington," he whined. "I'm not a rich man, I assure you. You'll ruin me!"

"Ruin you? What *do* you mean? I give you ten thousand pounds for one thousand and you say I ruin you! Really, it seems too ridiculously cheap. If you don't settle quickly, Mr. Cater, I shall raise my terms, I warn you!"

So it came about that Dorrington and Cater took cab together for a branch bank in Pimlico, whence Dorrington emerged with one thousand pounds in notes and gold, stowed carefully about his person, and Cater with the codicil to his uncle's will, which half an hour later he had safely burnt.

VI

SO MUCH FOR THE FIRST half of Dorrington's operation. For the second half he made no immediate hurry. If he had been aware of Samuel Greer's movements and Lugg's little plot he might have hurried, but as it was he busied himself in setting up on a more respectable scale by help of his newly-acquired money. But he did not long delay. He had the attested copy of the codicil, which would be as good as the original if properly backed with evidence in a court of law. The astute Cater, wise in his own conceit, just as was his equally astute cousin Flint, had clean overlooked the possibility of such a trick as this. And now all Dorrington had to do was to sell the copy for one more thousand pounds to Jarvis Flint.

It was on the morning of old Jerry Cater's funeral that he made his way to Deptford to do this, and he chuckled as he reflected on the probable surprise of Flint, who doubtless wondered what had become of his sweated inquiry agent, when confronted with his offer. But when he arrived at the ship-store shop he found that Flint was out, so he resolved to call again in the evening.

At that moment Jarvis Flint, Samuel Greer, and Lugg the lawyer were at the house in Bermondsey Wall attacking Paul Cater. Greer, foreseeing probable defiance by Cater from a window, had led the party in by the wharf door and so had taken Cater by surprise. Cater was in a suit of decent black, as befitted the occasion, and he received the news of the existence of a copy of the codicil he had destroyed with equal fury and apprehension.

"What do you mean?" he demanded. "What do you mean? I'm not to be bluffed like this! You talk about a codicil—where is it? Where is it, eh?"

"My dear sir," said Lugg peaceably—he was a small, snuffy man—"we are not here to make disturbances or quarrels, or breaches of the peace; we are here on a strictly business errand, and I assure you it will be for your best interests if you listen quietly to what we have to say. Ahem! It seems that Mr. Samuel Greer here has frequently seen the codicil—"

"Greer's a rascal—a thief—a scoundrel!" cried the irate Cater, shaking his fist in the thick of Greer's squint. "He swindled me out of ten pounds! He—"

"Really, Mr. Cater," Lugg interposed, "you do no good by such outbursts, and you prevent my putting the case before you. As I was saying, Mr. Greer has frequently seen the codicil, and saw it, indeed, on the very day of the late Mr. Cater's decease. You may not have come across it, and, indeed, there may be some temporary difficulty in finding the original. But fortunately Mr. Greer took notes of the contents and of the witnesses' names, and from those notes I have been able to draw up this statement, which Mr. Greer is prepared to subscribe to, by affidavit or declaration, if by any chance you may be unable to produce the original codicil."

Cater, seeing his thousand pounds to Dorrington going for nothing, and now confronted with the fear of losing ten thousand pounds more, could scarce speak for rage. "Greer's a liar, I tell you!" he spluttered out. "A liar, a thief, a scoundrel! His word—his affidavit—his oath—anything of his—isn't worth a straw!"

"That, my dear sir," Lugg proceeded equably, "is a thing that may remain for the probate court, and possibly a jury, to decide upon. In the meantime permit me to suggest that it will be better for all parties—cheaper in fact—if this matter be settled out of court. I think, if you will give the matter a little calm and unbiassed thought, you will admit that the balance of strength is altogether with our case. Would you like to look at the statement? Its effect, you will see, is, roughly speaking, to give my client a legacy of say about ten thousand pounds in value. The witnesses are easily produced, and really, I must say, for my part, if Mr. Greer, who has nothing to gain or lose either way, is prepared to take the serious responsibility of swearing a declaration—"

"I don't believe he will!" cried Cater, catching at the straw. "I don't believe he will. Mind, Greer," he went on, "there's penal servitude for perjury!"

"Yes," Greer answered, speaking for the first time, with a squint and a chuckle, "so there is. And for stealin' an' suppressin' dockyments, I'm told. I'm ready to make that 'ere declaration."

"I don't believe he is!" Cater said, with an attempt to affect indifference. "And anyhow, I needn't take any notice of it till he does."

"Well," said Lugg accommodatingly, "there need be no difficulty or delay about that. The declaration's all written out, and I'm a commissioner to administer oaths. I think that's a Bible I see on the shelf there, isn't it?" He stepped across to where the old Bible had lain since Greer flung it there, just before Jerry Cater's death. He took the book down and opened it at the title-page. "Yes," he said, "a Bible; and now—why—what? what?"

Mr. Lugg stood suddenly still and stared at the fly-leaf. Then he said quietly, "Let me see, it was on Monday last that Mr. Cater died, was it not?"

"Yes."

"Late in the afternoon?"

"Yes."

"Then, gentlemen, you must please prepare yourselves for a surprise. Mr. Cater evidently made another will, revoking all previous wills and codicils, on the very day of his death. And here it is!" He extended the Bible before him, and it was plain to see that the fly-leaf was covered with the weak, straggling handwriting of old Jerry Cater—a little weaker and a little more straggling than that in the other will, but unmistakably his.

Flint stared, perplexed and bewildered, Greer scratched his head and squinted blankly at the lawyer. Paul Cater passed his hand across his forehead and seized a tuft of hair over one temple as though he would pull it out. The only book in the house that he had not opened or looked at during his stay was the Bible.

"The thing is very short," Lugg went on, inclining the writing to the light. "'*This is the last will and testament of me, Jeremiah Cater, of Cater's Wharf. I give and bequeath the whole of the estate and property of which I may die possessed, whether real or personal, entirely and absolutely to—to—*' what is the name? Oh yes—'*to Henry Sinclair, my clerk—*'"

"What?" yelled Cater and Flint in chorus, each rising and clutching at the Bible. "Not Sinclair! No! Let me see!"

"I think, gentlemen," said the solicitor, putting their hands aside, "that you will get the information quickest by listening while I read. '—*to Henry Sinclair, my clerk. And I appoint the said Henry Sinclair my sole executor. And I wish it to be known that I do this, not only by way of reward to an honest servant, and to recompense him for his loss in loan transactions with me, but also to mark my sense of the neglect of my two nephews. And I revoke all former wills and codicils.*' Then follows date and signature and the signatures of witnesses—both apparently men of imperfect education."

"But you're mad—it's impossible!" exclaimed Cater, the first to find his tongue. "He *couldn't* have made a will then—he was too weak. Greer knows he couldn't."

Greer, who understood better than anybody else present the allusion in the will to the nephews' neglect, coughed dubiously, and said, "Well, he did get up while I was out. An' when I got back he had the Bible beside him, an' he seemed pretty well knocked up with something. An' the winder was wide open—I expect he opened it to holler out as well as he could to some chaps on the wharf or somewhere to come up by the wharf door and do the witnessing. An' now I think of it I expect he sent me out a-purpose in case—well, in case if I knowed I might get up to summat with the will. He told me not to hurry. An' I expect he about used himself up with the writin' an' the hollerin' an' the cold air an' what not."

Cater and Flint, greatly abashed, exchanged a rapid glance. Then Cater, with a preliminary cough, said hesitatingly, "Well now, Mr. Lugg, let us consider this. It seems quite evident to me—and no doubt it will to you, as my cousin's solicitor—it seems quite evident to me that my poor uncle could not have been in a sound state of mind when he made this very ridiculous will. Quite apart from all questions of genuineness, I've no doubt that a court would set it aside. And in view of that it would be very cruel to allow this poor man Sinclair to suppose himself to be entitled to a great deal of money, only to find himself disappointed and ruined after all. You'll agree with that, I'm sure. So I think it will be best for all parties if we keep this thing to ourselves, and just tear out that fly-leaf and burn it, to save trouble. And on my part I shall be glad to admit the copy of the codicil you have produced, and no doubt my cousin and I will be prepared to pay you a fee which will compensate you for any loss of business in actions—eh?"

Mr. Lugg was tempted, but he was no fool. Here was Samuel Greer at his elbow knowing everything, and without a doubt, no matter how well bribed, always ready to make more money by betraying the arrangement to Sinclair. And that would mean inevitable ruin to Lugg himself, and probably a dose of gaol. So he shook his head virtuously and said, "I couldn't think of anything of the sort, Mr. Cater, not for an instant. I am a solicitor, and I have my strict duties. It is my duty immediately to place this will in the hands of Mr. Henry Sinclair, as sole executor. I wish you a good-day, gentlemen."

And so it was that old Jerry Cater's money came at last to Sinclair. And the result was a joyful one, not only for Sinclair and his wife, but also for a number of poor debtors whose "paper" was part of the property. For Sinclair knew the plight of these wretches by personal experience, and was merciful, as neither Flint nor Paul Cater would have been. The two witnesses to the Bible will turned out to be bargemen. They had been mightily surprised to be hailed from Jerry Cater's window by the old man himself, already looking like a corpse. They had come up, however, at his request, and had witnessed the will, though neither knew anything of its contents. But they were ready to testify that it was written in a Bible, that they saw Cater sign it, and that the attesting signatures were theirs. They had helped the old man back into bed, and next day they heard that he was dead.

As for Dorrington, he had a thousand pounds to set him up in a gentlemanly line of business and villainy. Ignorant of what had happened, he attempted to tap Flint for another thousand pounds as he had designed, but was met with revilings and an explanation. Seeing that the game was finished, Dorrington laughed at both the cousins and turned his attention to his next case.

And old Jerry Cater's funeral was attended, as nobody would have expected, by two very genuine mourners—Paul Cater and Jarvis Flint. But they mourned, not the old man, but his lost fortune, and Paul Cater also mourned a sum of one thousand and ten pounds of his own. They had followed Lugg to the door when he walked off with the Bible in hope to persuade him, but he saw a wealthy client in prospect in Mr. Henry Sinclair, and would not allow his virtue to be shaken.

Samuel Greer walked away from the old house in moody case. Plainly there were no more pickings available from old Jerry Cater's wills and codicils. As he trudged by St. Saviour's Dock he was suddenly confronted by a large navvy with a black eye. The navvy stooped and inspected a peacock's feather-eye that adorned the band of the hat Greer was wearing. Then he calmly grabbed and inspected the hat itself, inside and outside. "Why, blow me if this ain't my 'at!" said the navvy. "Take that, ye dirty squintin' thief! And that too! And that!"

A Note About the Author

Arthur Morrison (1863–1945) was an English writer and journalist known for his authentic portrayal of London's working class and his detective stories. His most popular work is *A Child of the Jago*, a gripping work that fictionalizes a misfortunate area of London that Morrison was familiar with. Starting his writing career as a reporter, Morrison worked his way up the ranks of journalism, eventually becoming an editor. Along with his work as a journalist and author, Morrison was also a Japanese art collector, and published several works on the subject. After his death in 1945, Morrison left his art collection to the British Museum, with whom he had a close relationship with.

A Note from the Publisher

Spanning many genres, from non-fiction essays to literature classics to children's books and lyric poetry, Mint Edition books showcase the master works of our time in a modern new package. The text is freshly typeset, is clean and easy to read, and features a new note about the author in each volume. Many books also include exclusive new introductory material. Every book boasts a striking new cover, which makes it as appropriate for collecting as it is for gift giving. Mint Edition books are only printed when a reader orders them, so natural resources are not wasted. We're proud that our books are never manufactured in excess and exist only in the exact quantity they need to be read and enjoyed.

Discover more of your favorite classics with Bookfinity™.

- Track your reading with custom book lists.
- Get great book recommendations for your personalized Reader Type.
- Add reviews for your favorite books.
- AND MUCH MORE!

Visit **bookfinity.com** and take the fun Reader Type quiz to get started.

Enjoy our classic and modern companion pairings!